I SURVIVED

A '70s CHILDHOOD

John Hawksworth

While all the stories in this book are true, some names and identifying details have been changed to protect the privacy of the people involved.

For Mum, Joan, Connor, Amanda and Blair.

Without your love and support

I would not have made it this far.

CONTENTS

ACKNOWLEDGMENTS

All but one of the events described in this little book of mine are true. All the protagonists, however, are purely fictional and written to drive through the stories.

The only one that is not true is the story of paintballing. It would have been impossible for our four friends to take part in such an event in nineteen seventy-seven. The first recorded paintball event took place in nineteen eighty-one, held by Charles Gains with his friends in Henniker, New Hampshire, in the United States of America.

The school in this book was real; it was called Bridgefield High School and was situated in Halewood. It is no longer there.

All the characters in this are fictional – they are mixture of different memories of my school days.

Any resemblance to living people is a coincidence. I never had a teacher who owned pigs, nor one that detested anything foreign.

I also need to thank my family for their patience and understanding during this whole process. I have ignored them far too much, and frequently taken over our living room preventing them from watching television.

Finally, thanks go to the whole congregation and staff at St Andrews church in Tuebrook, Liverpool. You have literally saved my life, and the work you do for the local community is inspiring.

1. Early Days

The village of Halewood in the early 1960s was still just that – a small collection of houses surrounded by farmland. The main thoroughfare is Church Road, which linked us to nearest neighbour Hunts Cross/Gateacre. If you followed the road heading out of the village it brought you to Hale and Widnes. There were only the local neighbourhood shops, no supermarkets. From the end of church road, facing the row of shops from left to right we had hairdresser, greengrocer, post office/ newsagents, a garden shed dealership, butchers, the wool shop and in the far right another grocer.

When I was born there, in the early '60s, it was

part of the borough of Lancashire, which later changed to Sefton and it now resides in the borough of Knowsley due to the myriad number of political boundary changes over the years.

Employment levels were reasonably high, thanks to the presence of Ford's motor factory providing much of the Halewood workforce with jobs. So, despite being based in Lancashire few, if any, of the residents had ever worked in a woollen mill much less worn a flat cap. So, that image that popped into your head of men in flat caps, you can forget it.

I was lucky as a youngster to grow up with a sense of freedom. My friends and I would leave our homes early morning and, on most days, wouldn't return until the evening to be fed by our parents. Nobody panicked because we were missing all day, nobody called the police because we hadn't been seen for an hour. Left to our own devices, we made our plans and entertained ourselves. Nobody got into trouble – much. All of us were more frightened at what our mothers would do to us than any threat the local village bobby could make. However, we were brought

2

up to understand what was considered acceptable behaviour and we all spoke to adults with politeness and respect.

We had one village copper until the early seventies; if he gave us a clip round the earhole the last thing we would do is to go home and tell our mothers. (I can hear the liberals and moral do-gooders screaming as I write, "That's assault." No, it's not – it's called keeping a couple of cheeky, disrespecting ten-year-olds in line.)

Eventually, this village bobby, along with his in-depth local knowledge, was pensioned off when the area expanded. A new police station was established at the top of Leathers Lane. We all liked him; he was a tough but fair copper who treated everyone with consideration and patience.

As well as our local shops, like all good villages we had two pubs: the Derby Arms at one end of the village and the Eagle and Child at the other. It was literally a five-minute walk from one to the other, but separated by so much more. The Derby was a relatively new establishment (in other words less than fifty years in existence) and was frequented by the members of the village who, to put it politely, were the main reason we now had a police station! It changed hands on a regular basis, usually every three to four years. Each new manager would come in thinking they knew how to make a success from the business, only to be replaced by the brewery a couple of years later. It wasn't their fault, and I'm sure all of them were more than competent at their job. However, they were fighting a losing battle against a pub that had been in the village since the fifteenth century. As a result, the Eagle had become firmly established in the psyche of the village. The Derby is now a block of luxury flats.

To this day, the Eagle and Child still retains its Elizabethan look, and for the price of a pint, the older of the regulars will tell you the stories that surround its history.

For example, it is held as a truth by the locals that King Charles I rested there when it was a coach house during the civil war.

It is also held as a universal truth by the locals that Paul Simon, of Simon and Garfunkel, called in en route to whichever station he sat upon to write *Homeward Bound*.

Oh, and let us not forget the ghost stories! The former landlord who can be found at three in the morning enjoying a pint and pipe even though he's been dead over forty years. There is also a small child, aged four or five, who wanders up and down the corridor between the bars. This is the ghost of the child of a previous landlord; the child died after a fall down the stairs from the living quarters above the pub.

There are many more, and we all have a favourite.

All around the walls of both bars, there were plate racks, filled with china crockery of varying sizes depicting various scenes of a country nature. One morning, the manager had come down to let the cleaners in to find every one of the plates had been turned around so that only the underside of each dish was visible. On questioning the cleaning girls, they informed him that it was probably Rosie. She was the former wife of a previous landlord who had been murdered sometime in the eighteen hundreds and would regularly appear – her favourite trick being plate turning. I can honestly say that in the years I have worked and drank in this public house, I have never seen anything supernatural.

I attended the local infant and junior school, St Nicholas Church of England Primary School. The buildings dated back to the seventeenth century and had been set up to provide an education for the children of the local farmers. It was a good school, run by a headmaster who was ex-RAF and carried his sense of duty and service into his style of education. All the teachers loved being teachers. When I think back, I was incredibly fortunate to have been educated by every one of them.

Major scandals very rarely shattered the peace of the village when I was growing up. Most usually involved husbands sleeping with the incorrect wife – nothing of which I understood at that age.

When I was seven, we had our first and only murder. Although in hindsight it was more likely manslaughter or even accidental death. Anyway, Peter and Richard were brothers – well that's what the grown-ups told us to avoid any awkward questions. They argued, Peter hit Richard who fell backward, striking his head against their marble fireplace as he landed. He died instantly. Peter was arrested, charged with murder and slowly went mad inside the prison. I have always thought he would have preferred to hang; however, capital punishment had been abolished a few years earlier. So, he ended his days in a mental institute instead, driven mad by guilt.

The only other major scandal was The Great Christmas Club Theft. Like most of the village, my dad worked in Ford's. Every year they ran a Christmas club, with each of the three hundred men in the department paying in a fiver a month. Remember, this is the mid-sixties, a fiver was a lot of money when the average wage was around thirty to forty pounds a month. So, three hundred lots of five pounds a month for ten months comes to a total of fifteen thousand pounds, plus any interest. Just to put this into perspective for any of you youngsters out there, that's the equivalent for its time to the price of four three-bedroomed, semi-detached houses.

On the morning the lads were due to collect their savings in time for Christmas, the treasurer had disappeared. When some of the workers visited the treasurer's home, they found a new family had moved in. The new owner informed them that the previous owner had left to start a new life in Australia. I'm sure the fifteen thousand pounds he took with him helped to give him a fresh start.

I had no idea at the time, and I only found out years later during a conversation with Mum. I still received my lovely new bike off Santa though.

In the late nineteen sixties, Ford's embarked on an extensive improvement agenda. This required an ambitious building programme; as a result a new housing estate was established. Everything changed; a new library, four times the size of the previous building appeared. It was also at this time that we received the new police station. It was also on the back of this in conjunction with the baby boomers of the nineteen fifties that another secondary school was built, and my friends and I would be the second-year intake.

Along with this also came an increased crime rate,

and our house was broken into for the first time, which was nice.

That was pretty much living in the early days of my uncomplicated life. I grew up with two other boys, friends that as years progressed became inseparable. They were both a couple of months older than me – Phillip Cross and Michael Charles Hensworth. We met when we were just two years old at the local toddlers' group and would soon become firm friends. As we grew up together, we soon became known to one and all; we did everything together and went everywhere as a group.

Each of our mothers knew each of us almost as well as they knew their sons. If one of us was in trouble, the likelihood was that the other two were as well. We came through infant school together, we moved into juniors in the same year, and we all started at the secondary school together. We were so ingrained as a set to the teachers that we were put together to play the three wise men each year in the annual school nativity. Brothers in arms we may well have been, wise we most certainly weren't.

However, unlike me, they both had brothers and sisters.

Phillip had an elder brother, Roger and a younger sister, Anna. Roger was four years older, and to be perfectly honest the most miserable, self-centred, egotistical person I had ever met – and this was before I even knew what half of those words meant. He considered us all to be little more than a nuisance that had to be endured and treated us all with scorn and contempt. Roger had no time for his brother and even less for any of us. He would speak to us as if we were the scum of the earth and from what Phillip told us he treated their parents in much the same way.

He believed himself to be better than the rest of us, and when he won a scholarship to Liverpool College, this was just fate confirming the fact. Towards the end of his time at the school, he was instrumental in ensuring the only competition to his becoming head boy got expelled. He fabricated evidence that implicated the other boy in some thefts that had occurred recently in the school. He also ensured that the evidence seemed to point to the boy's two closest friends as accomplices. So, with the field cleared Roger became head boy unopposed. As far as Roger was concerned it was all part of the game of life; he destroyed that lad's life without a second thought. Roger left school, went on to university, then to work in London. Once he started in full-time employment, he never returned home and other than the very occasional Christmas card you wouldn't know Phillip had a brother. He was, in all honesty, a complete shit.

Anna, Phillip's sister, on the other hand, was the complete opposite. She adored her big brother, and Phillip adored her. He would happily curl up with her and read to her when he was older. She loved his friends and thought we were quite the ensemble, and for our part, we liked her. She was bright and had a quick and ready wit that kept the family and us in fits of laughter. Like Phillip she was into her sports and particularly excelled in athletics, eventually going on to represent both her school and Merseyside at competitions. She was also bright enough to understand her limitations; Anna could compete at junior level for the school, but she knew she would never be good enough to compete at the top level. So, she worked as hard on her academic studies as she did on the running track. In later life she was hired by a local MP to run his office until he sadly died of a heart attack; she now runs her recruitment agency. We all liked her, and when she is home, she always gives me a call, and the three of us will catch up, spending most of the night laughing.

Phillip's father, Richard, was an engineer who ran his own business and had won many prestigious design awards. Unfortunately, work and the success of his business was everything to him, leaving at six in the morning and not returning until late at night six days a week. As a result, Phillip barely saw his father in these early formative years.

His mother, Margaret – or Mrs. Cross as we all called her – was a small woman who ran her household with a tight rein. She tended to be relaxed with all of us, but she had a line we would never step over.

Phillip lived around the corner from me in the next road, Michael lived on the same street as me, opposite our local patch of greenery known locally as

Halewood Gardens. It was here that the three of us planned our adventures together, talked about whatever was on our minds. It was here that we all got drunk for the first time after receiving our O-Level results.

Mike only had the one sibling, a sister who was much older than him by five years. She was a serious-minded person who even as a youngster had absolutely no sense of humour. Carol was the only person I knew who never laughed once during a single episode of Monty Python, Are You Being Served and Porridge. It was beyond all of us that she would sit and watch Fawlty Towers with a completely straight face while everyone around her was crying with laughter. Carol only had time for her schoolwork; she always maintained that life was a serious business, there was no room for fun. When she left the school, she went on to become a doctor. I can only hope that her bedside manner improved.

Mike's father was ex-services who now sold life insurance for a living. He was a pleasant man, for the most part, given to the occasional wild verbal outburst.

He was old-school, with very little tolerance for people who did not conform to his version of normality.

His mum, Sylvia, on the other hand, was the complete opposite. She believed people made mistakes, bad life choices, and had to live the consequences. She would never judge anyone because of who they were. She had a part-time job working in John Lewis in Liverpool city. She treated us all as though we were her sons.

My mother was the same, treating the other two as though they were the brothers I could never have. I discovered when I was older that she had almost died giving birth to me, and in those days medical science was nowhere near as advanced as it is now. She was determined to find me some decent friends, which is why she took me to the toddlers' group in the first place. There was no way I was going to become the stereotypical spoilt only child. To be fair, I never felt I was an only child, my friends became as close as brothers over the years.

The three of us grew up together in at a time when space travel was in its infancy, computers were still a rarity, and the internet was still a dream. If we needed information, we had to find a book.

In later years we would meet and become friends with another boy, Isaac. Our little circle of three would become four. Our mothers never batted an eyelid at this new addition; they just welcomed him in as though he had always been there.

When we were all eight years old we made an astonishing discovery. It was on a Saturday afternoon in the woods by Greensbridge Lane. This was a well-known play area, its main attraction being a pond that was barely three feet deep and twenty feet wide.

We were all playing around, skipping stones across the water when we were joined by a couple of girls around our age. After the initial discussion as to why they were there, after all this was a place for boys only, the usual type of verbal exchange took place, the one about why boys are better than girls.

The debate completed, we settled into each other's company and returned to the art of stone skipping.

Eventually, we all just sat around when one of the girls suggested a swim. Always up for a dip, we confirmed this was a great idea and we all stripped off and jumped in.

Once we came out, it was then that the three of us discovered why girls are girls and boys are boys.

After the initial stares around, we just lay on the grass to dry off. It was an age of innocence that we no longer have; none of us thought there was anything wrong in our actions or behaviour. Just to be clear, I still don't; we were eight years old, for heaven's sake.

Half an hour later we were all dressed and walking home together. Nobody questioned what we had discovered, none of us was particularly interested; at least not for another four or five years. It was a different time; sex was an unknown quantity at age eight. We didn't receive any form of sex education until the second year of secondary school – more about that later.

We would always be there for each other from a young age. We were there for Phillip when his parents split up, for Isaac when he was seriously ill, and for Mike when his father kicked him out – and they were there for me when my father let me down badly, as bad as it can get. The selfish bastard died.

It comes as a shock at any age for you to lose one of your parents, but when you're ten years old your father is indestructible. It's an event of earth-shattering proportions.

It was about a month earlier that Dad started to feel unwell, tired and generally lacking in energy. His doctor sent him to the hospital for check-ups, the diagnosis came back as chronic heart disease. Six weeks later his heart just stopped.

That wasn't supposed to happen until I reached middle age at least, or even older. Certainly not at the tender age of ten. At that age, your dad is going to live forever. He would be there to teach me how to chat up girls, take me out and get me drunk for my eighteenth birthday. Help me pass my driving test, then ban me from using the car after I crash it. Have that awkward conversation when I turned thirteen. Make the emotional but ultimately embarrassing speech at my wedding.

To be there.

Was I being punished by God for something? If so,

this seemed very unfair. And it certainly didn't sound like the God they taught us about in scripture lessons.

Life, I had just discovered, could be shitty.

And the rest of the world just carried on. How? Didn't the world realise what had happened?

The day after, against the express wishes of their parents, Mike and Phillip came calling. They just sat with me up in my room; they even cried a little. They had liked my dad; I suspected they would miss him almost as much as I would.

Mum kept me home until after the funeral. Mike and Phillip virtually became lodgers. They would turn up as soon as the school day finished and did any homework they had in my room. They even managed to talk their parents into allowing them to be at the funeral.

After the funeral, everyone came back to the house. Relatives I didn't even know we had would come up and hug me, saying how sorry they were. I remember thinking over the years that they couldn't have been that sorry. The only time I ever saw them after that day was at funerals and weddings. Later,

Mike and Phillip dragged me out – under my mum's strict instructions. We went to the park together. Little was said, it didn't have to be; my friends were there for me.

Over the next couple of weeks, they would call around and coax me into joining them in the latest venture. Again, at the insistence of my mother, who had spoken to their mothers. Slowly over time, things gained a sense of normality.

It took me some time to get used to the idea that Dad wasn't there anymore. I would see something funny on the TV, or something daft happened in school and I would think, *I must remember to tell Dad about that,* only to then remember I couldn't anymore. These where the tough moments.

I was the first person in school to have lost someone, the first to go to a funeral. Which turned out to be quite a distinction; everyone in the school from the pre-schoolers through knew who I was. The teachers even took pity on me, and I didn't get any homework for the rest of the spring term. No more sweating over whether I was ever going to get to grips with algebra. Who cares how seventy years later the actions of the Victorians were still an influence on us in our day-to-day lives without us realising it?

Death, I began to realise was a two-edged sword. With that came a sense of guilt. Was it wrong for me to be happy? Should I be laughing at something one of my friends said?

But that is the point; life carries on. Regardless.

It didn't mean I loved Dad less.

So, I got on with my life and eventually, the pain lessened.

2. The Moon and Goodbye

Two spectacularly important events occurred in 1969. The first was my tenth birthday, on the sixteenth of July – finally into double figures. Turning ten is a big thing when you are only, well, nine. It's a big milestone going from a single into a double figure.

The second and less important occurred thirteen days later. Birthday celebrations had been delayed until this day so we could have a combined birthday/moon party. Mike and Phillip were staying over; we would all be sitting up to watch the moon landing. All of us sat in front of our small black and white set, mesmerised as we watched Neil Armstrong become the first man to walk on another planet. This was the greatest piece of history we had witnessed in our short lives so far. Others would come, but this was the first.

We had all heard how certain things occur in history, that have such an impact that everyone remembers where they were when they heard the news. We were babies at the time of JFK's assassination, so the moon landing in 1969 was our first experience of that feeling.

What impressed us about Neil Armstrong though, was that when he planted the American flag, he also placed his old Eagle Scout flag as well.

Now, I can appreciate that some of you out there are somewhat younger and have grown up where space travel is not that unusual. As a result, you may not grasp the enormity and significance of the event. To try and put it in perspective for you, even the most basic of mobile phones (you know, the ones that just text and make calls) have a larger memory than the any of computers used to send three men into space, successfully land them on another planet and then bring them back safely. So, it is impressive by 1969 standards.

Sat there at home, each one of us felt we were part of it all.

The only downside was the constant stream of new and useless facts our teacher thought she should impart to us as part of our science lesson on a Thursday afternoon.

For example, the moon's day is twenty-nine and a half hours long. It takes the moon a little more than twenty-seven days to orbit the earth. Did you know that it was considered bad luck to dig a grave or bury someone during a full moon? That chickens lay more eggs when the moon is in its final quarter? Why did she think we needed to know this information? Did she suspect the whole class was suddenly indulging in late-night spontaneous grave digging?

As I was now ten, this would be my last year in primary school, another minor milestone in my young life. The three of us would be moving on to 'big' school. It meant we had to conform to the old school traditions, including performing at the end-of-year extravaganza.

In a change to the previous rules, where we just

did whatever the teacher decided we would do, the class had a say in the content of this performance. It was a golden opportunity. We could recreate some of our favourite comedy sketches. Or we could just chicken out and do a nativity play like every other year.

We chickened out.

The traditional nativity it was, then.

I managed to secure the lead role of Joseph. An inspired piece of casting in my opinion. Mary, my bride-to-be, was to be played by a girl who considered herself the greatest actress the school had ever seen; she had taken the lead in all our school shows. She was not happy I would be filling the role of her prospective husband. Just to be completely clear, she was an absolute bitch about it.

It did not go well on the night.

Mary was throwing a tantrum because people were not taking it seriously enough; the shepherds were refusing to get changed into their costume, the wise men were frantically searching for the gifts, which they had lost, and the innkeeper had wet himself in a case of pre-show nervousness, which we all found hilarious, including me.

Things did not improve when we went live. The shepherds visited the baby Jesus in their school uniform, and the wise men presented him with a packet of rich tea biscuits, a pencil sharpener, and an inkwell. The crowning glory, however, has to be awarded to the innkeeper. When Mary and Joseph turned up he promptly told them he had one room left, which Mary was welcome to, however, and I quote, "Your husband can piss off." As a result, Joseph ended up having to gate-crash the birth of our Lord and Saviour.

Fortunately, the class only had to put up with the resultant embarrassment for two days, when we finished for the Christmas break, our first without Dad. Uncle Alan had invited us to spend Christmas with him and his family. Mum had accepted, deciding this might make it easier for both of us. Unfortunately, Uncle Alan was as mad as a box of frogs. I don't mean that in a jolly, laugh-out-loud Billy Connolly way. More like a 'Norman Bates without the homicidal tendencies' way.

My uncle had spent most of his life in the army; even though he had left he still ran his life and the household as though he was still serving, and we were his raw recruits.

As a result, kids were up at seven in the morning for thirty minutes' exercise followed by breakfast. At some point the previous day Uncle Alan would have worked out what jobs needed doing; these would be shared out between everyone, the requirement being that they were completed before lunch. After the required hour of sitting still and reading a book while our lunch settled, anyone below the age of sixteen would be thrown out to 'enjoy the fresh air'. Regardless of the weather conditions – "Fresh air is good for you!" he would bellow over my protests.

Uncle Alan had three kids; the two boys he treated as though they were the second coming, and a daughter he treated as though she was responsible for the fall of man.

The lads could receive bad school reports, low marks in their end-of-year exams and that was fine.

His daughter, on the other hand, was expected to be a straight-A student, anything less was unacceptable. Unfortunately, Sarah – his daughter – was not the cleverest of people, and even working at her best would manage B+ at best.

Years later I was told how at one parents' evening he apologised for her poor performance to each of her teachers.

Her mother, Aunty Jane, was completely ineffectual, having had any fight crushed out of her after years of being married to Uncle Alan. As far as my uncle was concerned, when they married Jane became his personal property to do with as he wished.

Sarah committed suicide when she was fifteen.

Christmas Day only got better after this one, so maybe there was a method to Mum's madness. Anyway, I was glad to be back home after a week with this lunatic uncle.

Another traditional event in our last year at school was the class weekend away. There was never any point in wondering where we might go; it was always London. We always stayed in the Baden Powell

House, which in the late sixties was run as a hostel for schools and members of the Scout Association.

We dumped our bags in one room and then headed across the road to the British Museum. None of us had ever been to London or the British Museum before, so the sight of a full-sized model of a blue whale hanging from the ceiling upon entry was something of a spectacle. I've had a love affair with whales ever since, but the blue whale is king of the whales.

I discovered that day that they aren't blue – they are a light grey and mottled white colour that makes them appear blue in the water. Its full Latin name is *Balaenoptera musculus* – which as a ten-year-old I found unpronounceable. We spent the best part of five hours there and still didn't get around everything.

The three of us could share a dorm, so we didn't get a lot of sleep.

On Saturday, Westminster Abbey beckoned. History was the only subject I excelled in; I coped with everything else – but history was different. Now, here I was, stood in the presence of some of the greatest figures from our history. Anyone of distinction was buried here. Kings, queens, politicians, writers, and poets. Although a certain playwright from Stratford-upon-Avon is conspicuous by his absence.

St Paul's is a beautiful building; however the abbey is an architectural work of genius (or so it said on one of the information stands). The same stand informed us that the building had been commissioned by Edward the Confessor in 1040, and was consecrated in 1045. The confessor king's remains are entombed in the front the high altar.

In the afternoon we went off to the Tower of London. The ravens were good; the crown jewels were being cleaned so I never got to see them. Best of all, we could swear in front of adults because of its other name, 'The Bloody Tower'.

I was now suffering from sensory overload with the amount of information and historical facts I was receiving.

William of Normandy, soon to be known as the conqueror, was so pleased to be passed over for the English crown in favour of his cousin, Harold, that he decided to congratulate him in person. Therefore, on

14th October 1066, he popped over to offer his warmest felicitations. After a rather heated conversation, they reached an agreement and William was crowned king on Christmas Day that same year.

Being a new king, he immediately embarked on an ambitious building programme – mainly to ensure no-one did what he'd just done to his cousin. On the banks of the River Thames stood an old Roman fort. William had this pulled down and, in its place, twenty years later, stood the Tower of London. I appreciate that twenty years seems a ridiculous length of time to build this edifice, but builders were a lot quicker in those days.

Not only was this a brilliant defence against foreign invaders, but it also turned out to be the perfect location for some of William's less agreeable friends. The very first guest was the Bishop of Durham, an extremely unpopular person with just about everyone. However, his life inside the Tower was quite comfortable through the judicious use of bribery. In February 1101, being the thoughtful and gracious person he was, he held a party for all the guards. Once he had got them all well and truly drunk, he walked out of the Tower and escaped with all his money.

Over the next eight hundred years, the tower became a bit better at law enforcement and played host to numerous kings, queens, princes, princesses, religious leaders, politicians and the occasional anarchist who had a serious disagreement with parliament.

We headed home the next day when another motorist thought we would find it hilarious if they rammed the back of our coach, shattering the window and sending glass splinters everywhere.

During the final week in junior school the whole class was taken on a trip to see our new secondary school. The first striking feature was the sheer size of it. It was like a small town on its own. Not just that, it smelt funny. All new and fresh; there wasn't that musty smell we were all used to in our junior school. It felt strange and impersonal – and just a little bit frightening.

We were split into smaller groups of six and

shown around by one of the school's teachers. I discovered that the teacher escorting my group was the head of the History department.

It took over an hour and a half to get around everywhere, before returning to the dining rooms for refreshment and a Q & A session. Some of the pupils were also there to answer any questions we might have.

Afterward, the three of us chatted and the most enthusiastic one among us was Phillip. He had been shown around the sports department and was, for all intents, in love. The sports hall had facilities to play any court-based game, there were two tennis courts outside as well as two football or rugby pitches, all-weather resources, and the Olympic-sized swimming pool. The school had the equipment to have a go at all the field and track events. Phillip thought he had died and gone to heaven.

At the end of that week the school held the end-of-term prize-giving. Michael won the English prize, Phillip received the sports prize and to my astonishment I was given the History prize. Mike missed out on the Maths prize to a lad named David Leots.

The following Monday we all attended the leavers' service in the local church, St Nicholas. It was a boring affair for a bunch of ten-year-olds. The vicar prayed for our future endeavours, the headmaster gave a speech about the future being in our hands, to grasp any opportunity that came our way and not to waste our potential.

Then, just as suddenly it was all over.

Junior school was finished with.

The great adventure of 'big school' awaited…

3. Meet the Educators and Macbeth

After the obligatory photograph of me in my new school uniform, the three of us headed off to start in the first week of September 1970 to begin our secondary education. I can't speak for the other two, but I was just a little nervous.

We were met at the school gates and directed to the courtyard. It was here that we got our first look at the headmaster, Mr. Brooks. There were around two hundred kids gathered as he welcomed us to his school and explained the procedure to allocate us to a class. To our surprise, the three of us ended up in the same form.

At first glance, the headmaster gave us the impression of a person who did not put up with any nonsense. Over the next eight years that first impression was only reinforced. Years later when we entered the sixth form, he would take us for a lesson every Friday morning – and our opinion would change over time.

Our class reference was L3, and our form tutor was called Mr. Jones – for continuity Mr. Jones would be our form tutor throughout our time at the school. He escorted us to our form room which seemed to be miles from the assembly point. The first task assigned to us was the completion of our timetables; while we completed this Mr. Jones continued to provide us with another set of rules. I was beginning to wonder how I was supposed to take all this in.

All the days consisted of the same format.

9.00am	Registration
9.15	Assembly
9.45	Lesson
10.15	Lesson

10.45	Morning break
11.00	Lesson
11.30	Lesson
12.00 Noon	Lunch
1.15pm	Lesson
1.45	Lesson
2.15	Afternoon break
2.30	Lesson
3.00	Lesson
3.30	Lesson
4.00	Home

The school was laid out in the shape of a square lollipop, for want of a better description. The main square surrounded the courtyard where we had all assembled on that first day. Each block had two floors, and the north block consisted of the Woodwork, Metalwork and Domestic Science classrooms on the ground floor with the science labs above.

On the left in the west block were the Music and Art departments downstairs, and the Maths, English, and Geography classes on the upper floor.

Opposite in the eastern block the History and Humanities departments presided over the kitchens and dining rooms.

The south block contained the administration offices, as well as the head and deputy head's office separated by the secretary's office. On the upper level was where the teachers' lounge sat. Halfway down this block another corridor led off to another music room on the right, with a state-of-the-art drama theatre on the left. Further down on the right was the entrance to the squash courts, then the changing rooms for PE. At the bottom, to the right was the entrance of the swimming pool and associated changing rooms. The sports hall was accessed opposite on the left.

Since the loss of my dad, this event was the biggest and scariest change I had encountered. It was all so different, and I no longer had the same teacher for all my lessons; I didn't live in one classroom anymore. I would be expected to find my way around the school unaided, and find the relevant classroom. In that first day, I had an hour of Maths in the morning, followed by an hour of English and History in the afternoon. It took all three of us a good proportion of the time to find the classroom to receive our education. Although the loss of time did not seem to be a problem, as the teachers made up for it with the amount of homework they provided us – and this was only our first day. Every time we met a new teacher during that first week, we would receive more information along with another set of instructions. By the end of the first week, we were even more confused than we had been at the beginning.

The second week wasn't much better.

In the third week, we only got lost once.

By the end of the fourth, it was as though we had always been at the school.

I had my share of brilliant teachers, as well as a few with some eccentricities. Mr. Burgess, our Geography teacher, had a deep dislike of all things French and preferred the company of his two Vietnamese potbellied pigs. If on any specific day none of us cared to hear about mountain formations or the continental drift, one of us only had to make a praiseworthy reference about something French, or ask, "How are the pigs, sir?" Once uttered the rest of the lesson would descend into a vitriolic diatribe as to why Britain was the greatest country in the world or a speech about why pigs are friendlier and more trustworthy than ninety-nine-point-nine percent of people.

Our four PE teachers were mostly reasonable, except for Mr. Arlington who took us on a Monday morning and was, we decided after one History lesson, descended from the Marquis de Sade. What sort of person, who has the responsibility of young bodies and minds, thinks it is fun to make us run a three and a half mile cross-country? A happy event that took place regardless of the weather conditions. Every Monday morning at 9.45 rain, hail, sunshine, snow or typhoon he would send us on our way to run around the village, much to the entertainment of the locals. Meanwhile, he would return to the office for a lovely hot cup of tea. I have no problem with sports and people who enjoy them in their many forms. I enjoy watching the occasional game of football, I never miss the Six Nations and I have even been known to partake in the odd game. However, I have no concept of what makes a normally sane individual voluntarily run a little over twenty-six miles for fun.

As part of our curriculum, we were required to take domestic science lessons (I believe these lessons are now called Food Technology) For the first time in our lives we were let loose in a kitchen, a strange and foreign land. Our teacher, the aptly named Mrs. Butcher, was shall we say, a well-built lady? She ran her little kingdom with a strictness that would have impressed any seasoned dictator, especially where the boys are concerned. Mrs. Butcher's philosophy – which she happily shared with us – when it came to the male of the species was, and I quote: "All men are bastards, and little boys are just bastards in training." One of the lads then rather stupidly pointed out that most of the greatest chefs were men. "That," she roared at the offender, "was just more evidence of the males' determination to ensure women had nothing to claim as their own, and just another way to grind womankind into the ground." I received my first ever detention for that remark, and my attempt at making custard was the only one with lumps in it. I only had her for the first two years as she moved on to pastures new. I cannot comment on her replacement as I gave this subject up in the third year, much to the relief of the catering industry I'm sure.

Mr. Benson, our Art teacher, was a fanatical Everton supporter. You could never be sure how you would be greeted on Monday, particularly if they had lost the previous Saturday. If there was any disturbance in his class, the three of us as Liverpool supporters could be guaranteed a night's detention. Derby weekends brought a different set of problems depending on who won; the Liverpudlians would have to keep their heads down if they had won, and we would receive no end of sarcastic comments if we lost. I want to be able to say what happened when Everton had a successful season, but I was only at the school for seven years.

In our third year, we had a new English teacher. Miss Sunderwell was tall, slim with long auburn hair that seemed to glow in the sunshine. She was not long qualified, but she was caring, gentle and understood us with a maturity that belied her tender years. This paragon of the education system held our attention with ease and we watched her every movement as she taught with a quiet authority. When she read a passage from whichever book we might be studying, it was as though an angel had entered the room. The three of us were not the only ones that had a small crush going on, after all this was in our third year and the hormones were running riot.

It was this wonderful woman who introduced us to the amazing (her description) world and incredible talent (again, her description) of the greatest living playwright, William Shakespeare. Miss Sunderwell had promised to take it easy on us and picked *A Midsummer Night's Dream*. There was an audible groan from the lads; we had hoped for something a bit gorier. *Macbeth* or *Hamlet* perhaps? Still, at least I was able to use all those things I'd learned as part of my Drama lessons.

Apart from his deep mistrust of American politicians, our History teacher, Mr. Donet, was almost normal. However, he was without doubt one of the best teachers I had, and I was lucky enough to keep him from my third year and throughout the sixth form. He encouraged me to think outside of the box, not to accept everything at face value, to look deeper – it was an invaluable lesson that has served me throughout my life. This attitude towards history and American politics was given some verification as the Watergate scandal unfolded.

Mrs. Harris was the poor unfortunate person charged with teaching me Maths. Fortunately, she had an unending store of patience; I will always be thankful for the extra time she put in with me to ensure I manged to scrape through my O-Level.

Mr. Brownlow, the Woodwork and Metalwork teacher, did not have the same aura of patience about him. The assumption was that he had clearly explained what was required and therefore we should understand and get on with the job. Mr. Brownlow would belittle any one of us that did not appear to be able to follow a set of instructions. Just one of the reasons I dropped both lessons when the time came to make our choices going into the exam years. The other reasons were around the fact that I appeared to only have thumbs on both hands when it came to anything DIY.

Our three science teachers for most of our time at the school were Mr. Baxter for Chemistry, Mr. Bowell for Physics and the delightful Miss Hansard for Biology. All these teachers could convey even the most complex of information in a clear manner. However, they each had their little quirks.

Mr. Baxter liked to finish off his classes by not only explaining, but also showing us what happened when you mixed the wrong chemicals. Which usually resulted in either nasty smells, smoke or explosions. The three of us hold him fully responsible for our suspension in the third year.

Mr. Bowell's little madness was a firm belief that no-one can call themselves educated in physics unless they had a clear understanding of Einstein's theorems.

Miss Hansard, we discovered, was a passionate follower of drag racers, even taking part in the odd one. Miss Hansard was also responsible for our sex-education – in purely academic terms, I hasten to add.

I rather think these lessons were an embarrassment for all involved.

Finally, there was the team of Mr. and Mrs. Foresman who job shared the drama teaching. Which meant that if one or the other managed to get an audition, the other could cover. As far as my recollections go, this never happened.

Both were completely bonkers. You had no idea what would happen as part of their lessons; a lesson about stage presence might suddenly tear off in a completely different direction. Lessons where chaotic and great fun. So much so, I joined their drama club. I was happy to take a back seat after the nativity fiasco of previous years. I would take a small part in the end-of-year extravaganza, however, in my final year of upper sixth these two had other ideas, and I ended up playing the lead in their adventurous production of *Macbeth*.

Naturally, I was overjoyed at the opportunity to humiliate myself in front of the whole school, followed by two performances in front of various school and local council dignitaries, and of course the usual mix of parents, brothers, sisters and assorted relations of the cast.

This was a serious change of direction, to put on a full-blown play, and not just any old play. Shakespeare is notoriously difficult for the best of actors, never mind a bunch of teenagers. In the past the end-of-year extravaganza had consisted of a mish-mash of contributions from the drama club, the music department, the odd aspiring singers, comedians and rock bands. The usual rehearsal period would be three weeks.

This was completely different. Three weeks was never going to be long enough. An opinion that was shared loudly by the drama club members with the teachers. I and the only other seventeen-year-old in the club also pointed out that there were only nineteen members, and *Macbeth* consisted of nearly forty characters. A shortfall of twenty-one.

It was then that it was made known to one and all, that some of us would have to double up, maybe even treble up, on roles.

We all remained sceptical.

However, both drama teachers agreed to increase the rehearsal time to four months.

Macbeth took over my life from that moment.

During the early period of rehearsal, I couldn't memorise a single word. Panic set in.

Also, we still did not have a Lady Macbeth!

A month later, a girl walked in and asked if she could join. Lady Macbeth had arrived. God bless her, she was really thrown in at the deep end and all credit to her, she, Susan, jumped in with both feet.

Over the next weeks things started to slowly come together. Three weeks before the live shows we had our first run through without our scripts. It went quite well, I even managed to remember about eighty per cent of my lines. Lady Macbeth, however, was word perfect. Turns out Susan had a photographic memory.

The next week we did a full dress rehearsal. Costume changes were kept at a minimum to make it a smoother and easier process. Lighting cues were settled upon; mood music was provided by the school orchestra. Everything seemed ready.

The next full performance was in front of the whole school. It went quite well, all things considered. A couple of lighting cues were missed, the witches' fire wouldn't light, and Macduff had to leave the stage to collect his sword for the big finish.

On the opening night, the nerves started with us all backstage as we heard the audience arriving. We all sat around quietly, as though waiting for our execution. Then we received the five-minute warning and the three witches left to take their place on stage.

Macbeth doesn't arrive until scene three of act one, so I stood in the stage wings with Banquo watching. We stole the occasional glance at each other, both of us as pale as each other. Then we heard the dreaded lines: "…and thrice again, to make up nine: – Peace! – the charms wound up." And on the two of us walked, and I heard a voice saying, "So foul and fair a day I have not seen," which surprisingly belonged to me. We were off and running.

Just as quickly, it was suddenly the interval. It flew over, or that's how it felt to me. Sprits were high backstage as we all thought it was going quite well.

Certainly, better than we thought it would.

The second half passed just as quickly. Before I knew it, Macduff had walked onto the stage carrying my severed head (full marks to the Art department, it was a frighteningly good likeness). Malcolm had made everyone an earl and invited them "to see us crown'd at Scone."

We did it all again the next night, then there was the after-show party. The only downside was the review written in the school magazine.

The editor had never liked me, or any of us really. He did not like the closeness the four of us had, the camaraderie of our friendship. So, he finished off his review stating, 'whilst the play was well staged, and well presented by the ensemble cast it was let down by the sadly lacklustre performance given by Macbeth.'

There you are then, that was the collection of the people charged with my education. While some of them, by today's standards were certifiably insane, I came out at the end with a fistful of qualifications. In their way, they were all good teachers. I was lucky.

4. Hi, I'm Isaac

In the mid-October of our second year of secondary education, a new lad joined the school and our class. Our form tutor decided that the best people to look after him would be the three of us; for some strange reason he thought we might be good role models. He came over and introduced himself. "Hi, I'm Isaac."

It can't have been easy for Isaac. After all, the three of us had known each other since we were two years old and had become a tight-knit group. The three of us did what was asked of us, although I wouldn't have said the responsibility overjoyed us. Three weeks later, and Isaac was still tagging along with us and slowly, through some form of human osmosis he became our friend; three became four.

Isaac's father, Benjamin Senior, worked as a retail manager. Having been offered a promotion, the whole family had moved to Liverpool and decided to decamp in our little village. He was a nice guy with a gentle sense of humour and the same mischievous twinkle in his eyes that Isaac had. I think he was relieved that Isaac had quickly found some new friends. He seemed to enjoy our company, he never judged us and often encouraged us in whatever madcap scheme we came up with.

Helen, Isaac's mother, didn't work. She considered it her job to look after her family. She too always gave us the odd word of encouragement; she loved cooking up little treats for us. There would always be a supply of tasty little pastries whenever we stayed over.

Isaac had an elder brother, Benjamin Junior, who was five years older than him. Ben Junior was great fun to be around; he never felt self-conscious about having a kick around at the local park with us kids, which is what it must have felt like to this seventeen-year-old.

Ben went away to university that following year, then went to teach in Israel. When war broke out, he volunteered and received a commission in the air force. He flew some combat missions. On one reconnaissance mission, he just vanished. No-one knows what happened; one minute he was chatting on his radio, the next he was gone. No signs of any wreckage were ever found, he just disappeared out of the skies. Isaac maintains that he is still alive, that one day there will be a knock on his door where he will stand, large as life.

On one Saturday all three of us received an embossed invitation to Isaac's Bar Mitzvah. So, on the appointed day I arrived at the synagogue, on Mather Avenue in the Allerton district of Liverpool, wearing my first ever suit.

We were going to be chaperoned by one of Isaac's aunties. Even though none of us were Jewish, we were still required to wear a skullcap as a sign of respect to God. However, we would not be allowed to sit with the main congregation, and we would sit in the area reserved for gentiles.

Isaac had some serious duties to carry out, a not too small part to play; he gave the blessing for that week's reading, he then read a passage of the scriptures specifically chosen by him. Finally, at the end of the service, he had to give a speech, which tradition dictates he begins, "Today I am a man…"

Once the formalities had been completed, there was a celebration party. There was a buffet with so much food on the table that it bowed in the middle, and every time a plate emptied, it was removed and instantly filled with a full one.

It was fun; there were these other people there who belonged to a strange and complicated group called girls. I had been informed that they also came from earth, but I didn't believe that. Phillip had confidence with girls that I never had; nothing ever worked out the way I had planned it. I knew what I wanted to say, but I would get within ten feet of them, mutter something inaudible, they would laugh, and I would then run for cover.

When we began a lesson about the atrocities committed during the Second World War, it was Isaac's dad who brought them alive and little too close to home for comfort.

Benjamin Senior was amongst the last of those Jews who were smuggled out of Poland in 1939, two months before the German war machine crossed the Polish borders. Hidden by the underground, he was secretly sent through Europe and into England, convinced with every step that it was only a matter of time before the Germans caught up with them.

It was many years after the war before Ben found out what happened to his parents, mainly through testimony to the war tribunals and witness statements made to the Jewish Holocaust Tracing Organisation.

Rosa and Heron, Isaac's grandparents, were allocated lodgings in the Warsaw Ghetto along with the other remaining Jews. That was around 1940. Life was not exactly fantastic, but at least they were alive and together. Heron, a musician, was assigned to manual labour. Food was scarce, but they had enough to survive in those early days. Their one hope was that they might be granted a travel visa so that they may eventually join their son in England.

Heron died first, stood at the street corner waiting for a friend when one of the German guards told him to move on. No-one has any idea what conversation passed between them; it didn't matter as the guards never needed any excuses when it came to teach a dirty little Jew his rightful place. Three of the guards began to systematically beat Heron with their truncheons, then tied his legs together, then to the back of a commandeered car and drove off, pulling Heron, his body never found.

Rosa waited two days before accepting that Heron was dead and moved in with her twin sister, Sarah.

When the ghetto had been cleared, most of the occupants ended up in the labour camps. Rosa and Sarah, however, were twins, and therefore subject to special status. Sent to a camp just outside the small village of Auschwitz, they were introduced to a charming doctor, a hero who had been decorated by the Führer himself, Josef Mengele.

The experiments began slowly at first; little tests to

see if they reacted to certain drugs in the same way. Mengele was fascinated by stories he had heard of telepathic consciousness between twins. If he could prove this theory and find a way to build upon it, it would be invaluable to the German war effort. Or at least that was his theory.

Now the experiments took a much more sinister aspect. One of the twins was thrown naked into a trench full of freezing water, and the other locked into a tin box which the guards slowly heated from outside. The doctors watched to see if the heat from one sister could be transmitted to the other. It is believed they survived that day, from then on details and testimony became unclear. Nobody can recall how they died.

Maybe it was through experimentation into the effects of high altitudes on the human body. For this, victims would be placed into a low-pressure chamber and the pressure then increased. Any survivors came out suffering from varying degrees of brain damage, making them useless for any other purpose, so they would go to the gas chambers.

Or they could have been drenched in the phosphorous used in incendiary devices to enable the doctors to test pharmaceutical treatments for burns.

Or, maybe they were forced to drink chemically processed seawater while being denied any food.

Or as a test subject on the effects of malaria.

Or the effects of mustard gas.

Or gas gangrene.

The list is long.

5. A Brief Stay in Hell

D ue to the diligence paid to our education at primary school, there was no real pressure on us in that first year of secondary school. We were all a year ahead of everyone else. As a result, we achieved consistently high results in all our studies, which made our parents and teachers happy.

However, it had the opposite effect on Daryl Brown and his circle of cronies, the Kavanagh twins. Daryl was a heavy, muscular kid even for an eleven-year-old. I managed to put myself in his sights. I never meant to; I hadn't even realised I had until it happened. It was during a History lesson, Daryl said something, and I laughed. I wasn't the only one – the whole class laughed, but Daryl only seemed to take offence at me.

Everyone got a telling off from the teacher, but that didn't satisfy Daryl's sense of injustice. He cornered me with the twins later that day. I took a beating, which I assumed would then be an end to the matter.

Apparently not.

From that day on they all decided that it was open season on me. They would follow me home at least twice a week, always on days when he knew my friends would be busy doing after-school activities. My father was dead, so they called me a bastard. I was also informed in graphic language why I was a waste of space, and in equally graphic language the I was a faggot. They would then go on to describe the various activities I would get up to with my other 'faggot' friends.

It wasn't just verbal abuse; there was physical as well. Thrown stones, punches, and they frequently tried to trip me up.

I tried to avoid him, I found several new routes

home, but they would eventually track me down, and the circle of abuse would recommence.

If you've never been through something like this, you can't begin to understand how it makes you feel.

It is degrading.

It's a form of mental torture.

I couldn't care less that Daryl acted in this way because of his insecurities, or because he was from a deprived background. It wasn't my fault that his mum and dad couldn't care less about him, or took no interest in his activities, that he was left to fend for himself most nights.

Anyway, what about his two assistants in all this? They didn't come from a deprived background. They came from a good, loving family and were well cared for.

So what excuses have you got for them, Mr. Psychologist?

It's simple – they were just a group of nasty little shits.

After the first year, thanks to my results I got

moved up a tier. So, I was rid of Daryl from my class. I no longer had to sit there feeling his eyes boring into the back of my head. I even joined the drama club after school to avoid him. Eventually, though, they would find me after a couple of weeks, and the torment would be worse – as though they stored it all up.

When we returned in September to begin our third year, it was with a sense of dread. I kept an eye out for them, but they were nowhere to be seen.

When I mentioned this fact to the others, I could tell from their mix of reactions that I was missing something.

Between all three of them, the full story unfolded.

Daryl's father only had one source of income – petty theft tied in with the odd drug deal. Daryl had decided that it was about time he took an active part in the family business. To prove he was ready, he planned to break into a local garage, steal whatever was available and sell it on. Through a mixture of threats and violence, he somehow convinced the twins to take part.

They met late one night outside the premises.

Access would be gained through the skylight in the roof. While the twins kept a lookout, Daryl shinnied up the drainpipe. He made it to the skylight when the roof gave way, and he plummeted fifty-plus feet to the waiting concrete below. The twins immediately did a runner as alarm bells sounded through the village.

Daryl was completely oblivious to this as he lay unconscious on the floor of the garage. The police arrived, called an ambulance and followed it to the hospital where they waited for him to wake up.

It took the police all of fifteen minutes to get him to tell the whole sorry tale. The twins got arrested that afternoon. They tried to protest their innocence, but it was obvious they were lying.

They were each sentenced to twelve months in a juvenile correction facility.

When they returned to the school, it was as three very different young men. The swagger and cockiness had disappeared.

6. Mishaps, Sickness, and

Misdemeanours

In the mid-seventies, the country was in the grip of a form of madness. While most national crazes tended to pass us by, this one had captured the imagination of at least one couple. Mr. and Mrs. Higginbottom, both in their fifties, had taken up streaking. For those not in the know, essentially, they went jogging in the nude. Better known the world over as streaking. There's even a song about it by Ray Stevens – look it up on YouTube it if you don't believe me. Mum told me over breakfast one morning that they had been seen heading up Rutland Avenue, which nearly caused me to choke on my toast.

I repeated this remarkable piece of information to the others on the way to school. They were equally as flabbergasted as I had been. We were all a bit slow; it was two days later that Phillip suggested a sleepover at Isaac's, who just happened to live in Rutland Avenue.

Isaac told us he had got a very suspicious look off his mum when he asked, but she said it was fine. Isaac mentioned he thought she might suspect what we had in mind. None of us were bothered if she did.

As it happened, they failed to materialise. Instead, the night was filled with games, snacks, fizzy drinks and laughter. So, we never got to see the Halewood Streakers – well, not that night anyway.

It was a couple of weeks later, on a Saturday night as we all walked home from the bus stop. There they were large as life – they appeared from around the corner, said, "Good evening, lads," and jogged on past us. After the initial surprise, we all descended into howls of laughter.

There were occurrences in our school days when none of us had the slightest idea what the teacher expected from us for a piece of homework that had been set that week. This lack of knowledge would require further investigation. It was thirty years before the internet; therefore we would have to consult things called books. These objects of knowledge gathered together in a building known as a library.

It was on one of these days that we all suffered one of the most frightening times of our young lives. The day started just like any other Saturday, there weren't any omens or portents written in the skies. We all thought Isaac was looking a bit off colour but did not give it any thought. Not until he turned very pale, vomited then slid off the chair and lay very still. Mrs. Gregson, the librarian, came running over, took one look at him and shouted at her assistant to call an ambulance.

Twenty minutes later Isaac was strapped to a stretcher with an oxygen mask over his very white face. As a precaution, the ambulance men insisted that we come with them to get checked over. Mrs. Gregson took all our telephone numbers, including Isaac's, assuring us she would contact our families immediately. These assurances made, we climbed aboard and were suddenly speeding through the village to the children's hospital in Myrtle Street, Liverpool. One unconscious and the other three scared out of their minds.

It was an hour later when all our parents arrived. Prior to this the doctors had taken our temperatures, prodded and poked us all over and taken a sample of blood for, as they put it "routine tests". Absolutely nothing about this struck us as routine.

It seemed a lifetime before the doctors gave us all the all-clear.

Isaac was still out cold. He had contracted a serious viral infection. His parents assured us the doctors were doing everything they could; but it was obvious from their expressions just how scared and worried they were.

The three of us could go home. The evening meal tasted like cardboard and laid heavy on the stomach. I know Mum and I watched some TV, I've no idea what though. I suppose I must have gone to bed at some point because when I woke up, that's where I was.

I'd only met Isaac some seven or eight months earlier, yet he had already become part of our extended family. In a short time, he had become our friend and fellow conspirator in all our adventures.

That Sunday was one of the longest I'd ever known. We all waited in Mike's for news. We mucked about, went for a walk at the insistence of his mother. Later, we decamped at mine, had dinner and continued to wait.

It was past eleven o'clock at night when the doorbell rang. Isaac's mum and dad came in, and they didn't need to say anything. The smile that lit up his mum's face said it all. Isaac had woken up just after eight-thirty that night. While the worst was over, he was still very weak. The three of us went a little nuts, whooping and dancing around the room with relief.

Isaac remained in the hospital for the next week; we wanted to visit, but it wasn't allowed in those days. We had to wait until he came home to continue his recuperation. Two weeks later he was given the all-clear and returned to school. Things very quickly returned to normal.

Most of our school holidays passed without any major incidents. The usual bumps and scrapes. However, during one school break after a particularly heavy downpour, we decided to indulge in one of our favourite pastimes. Called poly-bagging, it involved the use of a plastic bin bag, and a wet, muddy hill. Fortunately, we all had access to bin bags; the local park kindly provided us with the necessary hill. It was of a decent size, too. It took a good minute and a half at a reasonably modest speed to travel down to the bottom.

To take part, you need to climb into the bin bag, pulling it up around your waist, then sit down at the top, shove yourself off and slide down to the bottom. It is great fun. Well, it was when I was eleven.

On this trip, however, it turned out to be rather unpleasant. As I travelled full speed down the hill I travelled across water, mud, and grass and then a broken lemonade bottle which sliced through plastic, then through the flesh of my outer thigh.

An ambulance was called, and I was off to the children's hospital where I received a total of thirty-three stitches and a tetanus injection in my backside –

wrapped in bandages, I was sent home.

It was six weeks before the stitches could come out.

During our second year in secondary school we learned many a new and interesting fact, however, one fact we could all have done without learning, was the power of Mr. Jones' swing. It was one of the hottest summers of our childhood. Like any normal twelve-year-olds, we were never still, even in this hot weather. After a while, we decided it might be a good idea to splash some water on our faces to cool down.

I'm not sure which of us decided to throw the first bunched-up, soaking wet paper towel at the other, but it wasn't long before war broke out.

Feeling confined by the space in the boys' toilets, we invaded the corridor outside. We were having a great time. Unfortunately, the teacher on corridor patrol came around the corner just in time to meet the paper towel that had just launched. A little time later we stood outside our form head's classroom. Inside we could hear the explanation that was being made regarding our infractions of the school rules. Phillip was invited to join Mr. Jones; when he left, I was offered the same invitation. Inside I was given a lecture on what was considered acceptable behaviour in the school, why our recent escapade did not fit in that category. He then told me to bend over and gave six slaps with a slipper across the backside. It hurt like hell. Afterward we all congregated in the toilet to check the damage.

I have no complaints. We knew the consequences of our behaviour. A letter was issued to my mum informing her of what had taken place, and her reaction was, "Serves you right." She did not call the police screaming assault, Mum just looked me in the eye and said, "Serves you right," then grounded me for two weeks.

One Christmas when I was thirteen, I was rather astounded to receive the strange gift of a chemistry set. I have no idea why my Aunty Dorothy thought this was the perfect present. I mean, I was receiving chemistry lessons in school, but half the time I had no idea what the teacher was talking about.

Still, on Boxing Night I lay on my bed skimming through the manual when to my complete astonishment I found a set of instructions to make an explosive material. Upon checking the contents of the box, I was further astonished to find they had also provided the necessary ingredients.

It was the early nineteen-seventies, a different time. Terrorist activity was nothing like it is now. The IRA set off the occasional bomb, but attacks were rare, and we didn't have anything like the regulations around health and safety that there are now.

The next day I shared this discovery with my friends, and we all firmly agreed this would be great fun to play with. We convened a little later that day on the local patch of green. Isaac had brought along a small polystyrene box, complete with lid, something one of his Christmas presents had come in. He thought it might be useful to help contain the expected explosion and perhaps reduce any noise. "Good thinking," we all said.

The instruction stated that once the final catalyst had been added it would take approximately thirty seconds for the chemicals to react with each other.

Excellent, this would give enough time to duck

and cover.

Following the instructions as closely as a bunch of excited thirteen-years-olds could, we added the ingredients to the polystyrene holder. Mike had the lid ready to slam down, I added the final ingredient, the lid went down, and we ran for cover. Approximately thirty seconds was exactly that. It took a bit longer and thinking it had not worked we all made to go over and check. As soon as we made that decision there was an almighty bang, the container disintegrated, and it started to rain little polystyrene balls.

Thankfully it had snowed the day before, so by the time doors started to open the resulting rainfall had magically blended into the wilderness. Feigning innocence, we looked around with puzzled expressions, as though we too were wondering where the noise had come from. I have my doubts that anyone was convinced by our pretence.

The front doors soon closed once people realised there was nothing to see. Meanwhile, we all considered the experiment a huge succes, if a little volatile.

During the next couple of weeks, we continued

with our experiments away from prying eyes. Over this period neighbours could often be heard discussing the strange bangs heard every couple of days around the village. One person went so far as to suggest that the quarry over in Cronton may be operating again. None of us felt it was our place to question this assumption as we continued in our quest for knowledge.

We blew up anything we could get our hands on; Lego and Mechano constructions died at the altar of our scientific advancement. Within a few months, we had become so proficient that we knew exactly the proportions required to blow an Action Man's head clean off his shoulders.

Of course, this could not go on forever. It had to end one day. That day was a Thursday afternoon when, impatient to test our latest experimental batch, we had a small incident in the school science lab.

Every Thursday, our final lesson of the day was Chemistry. Once the lesson had finished, Mr. Baxter would dismiss us, and he would immediately head out the door.

Taking advantage of this fact, we loitered around

until everyone had left. Mike grabbed a large glass beaker. Between us, we added the ingredients. Phillip dropped a golf ball in, saying that he wanted to see how far it would go.

It was probably at this point that the inner alarm bells should have started ringing in our heads. Unfortunately, the batteries weren't working.

Adding the final ingredient, we all ducked for cover on the other side of the room. We just made it when there was an almighty bang, followed immediately by the sound of breaking glass, and then by a dull 'thunk' noise.

We all stood up to survey the damage, looking at each other with the realisation of what we had just done. Then the classroom door opened, and the headmaster came in. The beaker was in pieces across the lab desk, the classroom window behind the desk had been blown out and the ceiling now contained a firmly embedded golf ball ornament.

The head looked at the three of us, pointed out the door and said, "My office, now."

It was the second time we received corporal

punishment; this time it was accompanied by a two-week suspension. Our parents stopped all pocket money until the damage we had caused had been paid for.

By the end of my two-week suspension, I can state in all truthfulness that we now owned the cleanest house in Halewood. It positively glowed.

All of us had a fairly stable upbringing; any misdemeanours were through nobody's fault but our own, and we were, quite rightly, severely punished for them. However, for Phillip and me that stability was upset, for very different reasons.

In my circumstance, it was when Mum started dating again. Most of the guys she went out with lasted a couple of dinner dates, then were gone. Except for one, who managed to stay the course for almost eight months.

He appeared on the scene slowly. Mum would have a night out when I was having a sleepover at one of my friends'. Mum met him on one of those nights out. They had a couple of meals together, then Mum invited him to ours for dinner one Wednesday night.

He was the opposite of Dad, which may have been the point for Mum.

For a start he was, as he put it "between jobs". I'd never met a grownup who didn't work. That's what grownups did. When I asked him why he did not have a job, he said he was "considering his options". He said he did not want to work in an office having the life sucked out of him by "the man". Then he went off on this weird speech about the corruption of the masses by the establishment, hippy-type thing. I wasn't really listening by the end.

He wanted us to be friends; I told him I had plenty of friends, thanks.

That didn't stop him from trying to involve me in one activity after another. I could escape most of them by stating I had a mountain of homework to get through. Once he told me that qualifications were just another way of the establishment attaching labels to people to keep them in their place.

However, I couldn't escape all the time. I missed out on a paintballing event because 'Tommy' had managed to get tickets for the Liverpool home game, even though he was aware I had very little interest in football.

These little plans would take place on a lot of Saturdays. I was spending more weekends with him than with my mates. I didn't dislike him, I tolerated him. Then he stepped over the mark. He announced he had made all these plans for the following weekend. I told him I was at Scout Camp. His response was, "Not anymore, kiddo." Apparently, he did not approve of pseudo-paramilitary organisations.

That was the turning point. He was starting to take me away from everything I enjoyed. I didn't get what Mum saw in him. He dressed like a guy stuck in the sixties, as if he had joined the flower power generation and forgot to move on.

It became awkward whenever he turned up; I would be polite as was expected, but it was becoming obvious that I considered him a prat. Then, not long after the science lab incident he just stopped coming around. I asked Mum about it, she just said it was over, that she had had enough of him. She asked if I missed him being around. I told her I did not and that it had felt like he was trying to take all the things I liked away from me. Mum told me she hadn't realised I felt like that, and I should have said something.

Apparently, I found out a couple of months later, that they had had a massive row. It had been about the explosive episode and my suspension. He had called me a spoilt brat, that I didn't appreciate the things he did for me. The breaking point was when he said he was going to take his belt to me over the whole school occurrence. That's when Mum gave him his marching orders.

Last I heard, he had buggered off to live as part of a commune in Wales.

For Phillip, the family crisis took a different route. He found out his dad was having an affair with his secretary.

Phillip saw them in the city centre when he was looking for a new set of football boots; they were parked up and his dad was kissing another woman. He kept this to himself for a few months, then one afternoon he told Mike he thought his dad was having an affair and told him what he had seen. Phillip was upset, confused and conflicted as to whether he should tell his mum. What did he say to his dad? Their relationship was never great to begin with due to the long hours his dad worked, but this was something else entirely. What if he told his mum and then they split up?

This was a world of adults that none of us understood. We were all thirteen; the world of adult behaviour was still a mysterious foreign land. Mike suggested Phillip should get the opinion of another adult. Naturally Phillip was reluctant to share this with anyone else.

That's when they turned up at mine. It was obvious from the look on their faces that something was wrong. When they told me, he asked if he could talk to my mum about what to do. Phillip has always had, and still does, a huge respect for my mum and her ability to see to the centre of a problem and come up with a viable solution.

So that's what he did. Afterwards, Mum told Phillip not to do anything, she would take care of it. The look of relief on his face spoke a thousand words. Mum also made sure that Phillip understood this was not his fault, that the only person to blame in this situation was his dad. Whatever happened next, he had to understand that. He should never have been put into this situation. I don't know how Phillip had lived with this information without saying anything for over four months.

None of us know what Mum did, apart from speaking with Phillip's mum. We have no idea what was said between them. I gathered from Mum a few months later that the news had not been a huge surprise to her. Apparently she had suspected as much for a while. Anyway, whatever was said, Phillip's dad left the family home the next day.

Phillip saw his dad from time to time over the following months; it took a long time for them to rebuild their relationship. Phillip was inclined to never see him again, until I said he was lucky to have his dad around. I think that made them all understand just a little bit what the previous three years had been like for me.

7. *When Scouts Ruled the World*

Summer holidays always meant Scout camp. The Scouts played a big part in our youth. All three of us had come up through the Cubs. Later, Isaac would join us.

Scouting taught us self-sufficiency, taught us to stand on our own two feet. We learned a set of values and skills about honour, duty, and service to others that have stood the test of time. Even though modern society seems to consider such values out of date and something to be scorned, a source of ridicule.

Not only that, we learned how to organise and carry out a set of plans; to be able to adapt when those plans did not go as expected.

We learned how to pitch a tent, make and cook a meal on an open fire, how to use knives and axes safely and responsibly. To abseil, rock climb, canoe and how to read a map.

During my time in Scouting, I saw most of Great Britain as well as France, Belgium, Holland, Germany, and Luxembourg. During the spring and summer, we would be away spending one weekend a month living under canvas. In the autumn and winter months, we stayed in youth hostels or camped.

Scouting was responsible for my discovery of Jazz music. It was during the summer camp of nineteen seventy-two, in a place called Linnet Clough just outside Stockport.

We had been on a trip down the River Goyt; at the end of the journey we were left to our own devices to explore the market town of Mellor. While wandering around, passing by a country pub called the Devonshire Arms we all heard music emanating from within.

It wasn't like anything we had heard before. The

only music we had heard usually came from whatever Top of the Pops was showing that week. Growing up in Liverpool you tend to get overwhelmed by the music of the Merseybeat scene. The likes of The Beatles, Gerry and the Pacemakers, The Merseybeats, The Beatles, Rory Storm and the Hurricanes, The Beatles and... oh yes... The Beatles.

But this music was different. It was like it had a life of its own. Jazz, real live music. We pressed our noses against the windows in the hope of catching a better look. When someone opened the door, I slipped in; the others had no choice but to follow.

This was my first epiphany. I was in love. Although I would enjoy the Punk age in another four years, I would always come back to the Jazz. We all stood watching for about twenty minutes before someone noticed our presence, and this being the early seventies we had to be escorted out the door. The tune playing as we left, I learned later was called Sweet Georgia Brown, which is still one of my favourite pieces. I have been to a few Jazz and Blues concerts over the years, but this day will always hold a special place.

As I have already stated, this all occurred at our Scout summer camp in Linnet Clough. On the day of our arrival, there was already a Scout Troop set up. Once we had set our camp, they wandered over, heard the Scouse accent and immediately challenged us to a game of football. Naturally, we accepted their challenge, considering it a matter of honour.

Half an hour later, the ambulance sped off all sirens blaring and containing their Senior Patrol Leader complete with a broken ankle. It was a superb tackle though.

The only other lesson learned from this camp is that when cooking baked beans in their tin, it is imperative that you make a hole in the top to release the steam. Otherwise they are liable to explode, and you end up covered in baked beans and tomato sauce. Mind you, they do travel a fair distance in an upwardly mobile direction.

In another year, we all became experts at shovelling shit.

It was in a foreign land, where the language is of a strange nature – Anglesey, a Welsh province attached to the mainland via the A55 and the Menai Bridge. The site we stayed on that summer was home to a herd of cows for the rest of the year. Therefore, before we could pitch our tent, we had to remove the vast quantities of cow-pats currently occupying the area. It took us, and I'm talking about seventeen of us here, just on an hour to make the field habitable. Seriously, it was everywhere.

Then, once the tents were up, the traditional summer weather decided to appear. It was a torrential downpour, which led to another discovery about the field – its appalling drainage quality. Shovels out again, this time to dig trenches around the sides of the tents to direct the water away.

Despite these inauspicious beginnings it turned out to be a decent camp.

During our time there I learned to abseil. Standing at the top of a three-hundred-foot drop I was attached to a length of rope and a safety harness, then lowered over the side to walk down the side of the cliff. It was terrifying as I was lowered and then stepped off the edge, but once I was over it was great fun.

The four of us passed our canoeing exams, which entailed us proving we could get in and out of a canoe safely and we could escape the canoe if it overturned.

We even had a go at archery, however, based on our abilities, I doubt any of us would be invited to join Robin Hood and his Merry Men.

The only sour part of the camp, whenever we entered a shop, everyone around us immediately spoke only in Welsh. We were just kids on our annual Scout camp, and we did not feel very welcome when we needed to venture into the village for essential supplies.

With the above in mind, Skip decided to head in the opposite direction the next year. Auchengillan Adventure Scout Camp in Scotland. Numbers had started to reduce over the previous year; to get the numbers required we combined the camp with the Cubs.

As this was a specialist outdoor adventure facility, we had sessions in abseiling, climbing, rifle shooting and archery. Oh, and then there was the night hike, which Skip somehow forgot to tell us about – it was a surprise, he said.

Essentially we were all bundled into the minibus at ten in the night, driven around for an hour, then dumped in the middle of nowhere. Skip handed us a compass, map, and torch, then informed us, "You are on the West Highway, camp is fifteen miles away. Breakfast is at seven thirty," then climbed back in the minibus, bid us a fond farewell and we stood and watched as the lights of the bus disappeared into the distance.

The eldest amongst us said, "OK, let's not panic," so that's what we did. Panic, I mean. For a couple of minutes anyway, then some bright spark suggested we check the map. Good idea, we thought – so, who's got the map?

It turns out the chap who had taken the map off Skip had a sudden call of nature – so he nipped off to take care of business. He put the map down, then forgot all about until someone mentioned it.

Another few minutes were lost as we all took part in an episode of The Scouts and The Map Crusade. After this combination of panic, searching and having a strongly worded conversation with the map man, we realised that we now had absolutely no idea from which direction we had come.

So, we guessed. Wrongly.

We walked for about an hour and a half when we found a signpost indicating the direction to Auchengillan. Unfortunately, it was pointing back the way we had come.

Once again, a conversation was held with map man, then we headed back in the correct direction.

We turned around, and the hike progressed to plan. We walked, talked and laughed. Some of the older lads smoked, passing them around. They tasted disgusting. The walls and hedges received the ocasional watering as we went. As it turned out, we ate breakfast at eight forty-five, by which time Skip was ready to climb in the bus and look for us. Which was nice. At least it showed he cared.

The Cubs were invited by another Cub pack to go on a haggis hunt. The haggis is a notoriously shy animal, living on the tops of the mountainside. They are small, furry creatures with two long right legs and two shorter left legs. So, they run around the sides of the mountains in an anti-clockwise direction. Catching them is a simple task, the haggis being such shy beasties and easy to scare. The Haggis Hunter fires off his shotgun; this startles the haggis which jumps in the air, turns around and attempts to run in the opposite direction. However, now the two short left legs are on the wrong side, and consequently, the poor old haggis rolls down the side of the mountain to the bottom. All the Haggis Hunter must do is pick them up and pop them into his bag.

All true, honestly.

Every camp has its share of new Scouts. This year was no exception. Each one reacts to being away from home in a different way. Robert Leeford was a spoilt little brat. He decided that the best way to ensure he was still the centre of attention and to make sure everyone knew he was more important than anyone else, was to be as disruptive as possible.

By the seventh day, everyone had had enough. Fortunately, I was off-site when this event took place as it was my turn on kitchen duties. As a result, I was in the village with Skip picking up vital supplies.

Upon our return, as the bus turned the final corner and our site came into view, we were met with the sight of a stark-naked Scout, staked out face down with a bunch of daffodils growing out of his arse.

When the people you have been pissing off all week are fellow Scouts who have knowledge of skills you haven't, retribution can be swift and uncompromising. I was curled up in laughter; Skip went ballistic.

The rest of the day everyone found they were confined to tents. Skip had a go at the Cub leaders for not stepping in. They feigned innocence, claiming they had no idea what was going on. Eventually, everyone calmed down; Robert apologised to the rest of the Scout Troop for his behaviour and the Troop, in turn, apologised for their actions, saying it had not meant to get that out of hand. They just wanted to teach him a lesson. Robert was a model Scout from that day until camp finished the following week. However, he did not continue with the Troop.

Now we come to the camp that became the most adventurous and the most memorable of our Scouting holidays. Skip decided to do a mini-tour of Europe, taking in France, Belgium, Germany, and Holland with an unplanned visit to the Duchy of Luxembourg.

It would be our final year as Scouts; we would all turn sixteen over the next couple of months. We would either leave or start a Venture Scout Unit. At this point we hadn't made any decision.

We left at ten in the night, driving through to Dover for the six o'clock morning ferry to Marseilles. Sorry France, but Marseilles is a dump. The rest of your country seemed quite nice, Paris is lovely. Which is where we stayed first, in a youth hostel. We went up the Eiffel Tower, down into the basement of Notre-Dame Cathedral and along the River Seine. We visited the Arc de Triomphe – on arrival we did puzzle how we were going to negotiate the roundabout, which has five lanes. People have been lost forever in that spot, spending eternity circling the Arc de Triomphe. However, a fellow tourist took pity on us and pointed to the subway, which went under the roundabout. So, we decided to take that route instead, which brought us out directly under the arc; it was quite a sight.

With Paris visited, we headed off to Belgium and the city of Bruges. Beautiful place. We did two walking tours, one in the day and a night tour. We visited Market Square and – WOW – a museum dedicated to chocolate. Imagine it – a museum about chocolate. And they gave out samples. Sorry Liverpool and London, I like your museums, but you don't give out chocolate.

We also visited the Basilica of Blood, which – believe it or not – contains a vial of blood that is supposedly from Jesus.

Then, a lovely Belgian waffle lunch and a canal boat trip.

That was Belgium; onward and upward. Next stop, Germany.

We arrived at the campsite early in the morning, so elected to sleep in the bus and sort out camp when the sun was in evidence.

The people of Germany were incredibly friendly and welcoming. We made friends with the German

Cubs and Scouts who were sharing the site with us. Fortunately, they all spoke faultless English, as we didn't speak any German. We visited a couple of places, including Cologne Cathedral and water parks. We even managed to get a taste of German beer.

While staying in Germany, Skip realised that the border with Luxembourg was only a couple of hours' drive away. Seven o'clock on Wednesday morning we all piled into the minibus and headed off. It was worth it, although they do show a certain lack of imagination. The capital of Luxembourg is... well... Luxembourg. However, putting that to one side – a little-known fact. Before they finally gained their independence in eighteen sixty-seven ownership passed between the Belgians, Dutch, Austrians, Spanish, and Germans. The most famous incumbent to sit in power was the Duke of Wenceslaus, the father of the Good King Wenceslaus of the Christmas carol fame.

We left the camp reluctantly and headed towards Amsterdam and our four-day stay in a youth hostel.

It would prove to be the best part of the holiday.

It was our last night, and during the previous evenings we had become friendly with a couple of girls, and we would usually spend our time with them once the evening meal had been consumed. I had become friendly with a girl called Anya, who was already sixteen. As a secret smoker, this would require her nipping outside to light up, around the corner where she could not be discovered. I would usually go with her, and we would always have a quick snog before returning. On the last night, we went outside, she had her smoke, then we snogged as was the routine. Only we stayed out a bit longer than usual, I had assumed because this was our last night. We were out there for a long time, and when we eventually returned inside, I was no longer a boy – or a virgin.

The next day we went home, Anya and her group had already left. I never saw her again. And I've never forgotten her, or the smokey taste of her.

I must have had some smug look on my face because Skip kept asking me why I was looking so pleased. I suspect he knew exactly why.

Skip was the only name we had for our Scout

Leader. He did all this work with us on a voluntary basis – Scout Leaders at grass roots level don't get paid. Skip organised all these summer camps, the weekends away throughout the year and running the weekly Scout meeting and everything that involved while also holding down a full-time job.

He was a huge influence on all of us, a mentor and protector whenever we were away from our parents. He always had our back, and we never doubted that fact.

In later years we discovered that he would fund some of the costs for the less advantaged of the Scouts in his charge. No boy would miss out on a camp because of money. He sold football cards, the type you paid a pound and picked a team. The winner gets a fiver and the Scouts get fifteen.

We enjoyed his company, and he enjoyed ours. If we were home from university, we always called into the Scout Hut on a Thursday night. And Skip would immediately commandeer us to help, then join us for a beer afterward.

Sadly, he was taken from us far too early. It was a

testament to him and his character that nearly two hundred attended his funeral, most of them former Scouts like us. It was then that we found out his name was Graham, but to all of us, he will always be Skip.

8. What is going on?

So, as you now know, I lost my virginity a couple of months before my sixteenth birthday. Which brings me to the other overwhelming changes that we all, male and female, must survive. The weird and wonderful world of puberty.

Well, weird certainly – I'm not so sure about the wonderful.

To set the scene – sex education in nineteen seventy-two was basic at best, negligent at worst. I had a total of two one-hour biology lessons devoted to the subject, one of which was taken up by a thirty-minute animated film called Living and Growing. At the end of this film I knew what bodily changes happen to boys and girls, what was meant by a 'period', what an erection was, and its purpose in the act of sexual intercourse. The film never once referred to these changes as puberty, it was just called growing up, changing from a child into an adult.

That is the essence of my sex education in school.

The first time I heard the word 'puberty', I honestly thought it meant that I would get to go to more parties. It turned out that what it meant was that I would turn into moody, argumentative bugger who required food and sleep twenty-four hours a day for the next four to five years.

Information that I was never told included the fact I would need to shower three times a day as my body turned into a professional sweat producer. From age thirteen onwards I was sweating from glands I didn't even know I had. Never had my underwear become a physical part of me that would require a great deal more effort to remove. I was used to being hot and sweaty after physical exercise, now I could break into a sweat just by sitting down, standing up, walking across the road or by standing completely still. My conclusion was that girls got the period, boys got extra sweat glands.

Then there's the effect this had on hair texture – and I don't mean in a nice way. It was as if someone sneaked into by bedroom in the night and emptied the contents of a chip pan over my hair.

They never mentioned that the hormone release would result in breast growth. By age fourteen my breasts wobbled whenever I took part in sports. The growth in my case wasn't even that excessive, a couple of other lads in our year carried a magnificent set until they were about sixteen.

Then, there's the random growth spurts. One part of by body would suddenly decide to grow faster than the rest – for several months I appeared to be all legs. I lost all coordination; walking without falling over was a challenge, never mind sport. I couldn't kick a ball or run in a straight line. Swimming became a major challenge which must have been hilarious to the spectator. For a while there whenever I entered the school swimming pool, I looked like I was having a fit.

Next there are the changes to a boy's voice. One minute I would sound like Darth Vader, the next I was doing a reasonable impersonation of Mickey Mouse. Oh, and those weird sounds don't happen in the privacy of a quiet chat with family or friends. Oh no, it's much more fun if it happens during your turn as the reader for the morning assembly in front the whole of the fifth year; or in front of your classmates during your English oral presentation about the merits of Holden Caulfield from J D Salinger's *Catcher in the Rye*.

Let's not forget the other most precious gift of puberty – zits, spots, and pimples – or acne as it likes to be called. Suddenly, overnight the whole school broke out in spots and generally terrible skin conditions. At one point I had a spot on my backside that was so big I thought I was growing a third buttock. It was as if a plague had infected the whole of the third-year male population. Only one lad seemed to escape this curse, Robert his name was – or "The Carrier" as we liked to think of him.

Even though I experienced an accelerated rate of

hair growth in new and interesting body locations, there was only one set I awaited with increasing impatience. My first pubic hairs arrived at age twelve, just a couple of weeks before my thirteenth birthday. I wasn't impressed; I expected to wake up one morning with a full, bushy set of pubic hairs. These were fine with a very soft and downy feel to them. Naturally once they arrived, their progress needed to be checked on a regular basis. During the morning shower, getting changed out of school uniform when I got home. I even managed to occasionally slip in an extra check during the day – getting changed after PE was useful for that.

Another interesting phenomenon that no-one warned me about were the sudden, inexplicable, spontaneous erections. For no reason whatsoever, I would abruptly get an erection. This was fine when alone, or even at home where I could employ the judicious use of a cushion until things calmed down. Not only did I look like a drowning fish in the pool, I now had the occasional unasked-for rudder for steering assistance – which is fine until you must do backstroke when it looks like you have a periscope in your trunks.

Our sex education classes reliably informed us that erections only occurred during sexual arousal, as a preparation for intercourse. This also caused some confusion, especially when I had a spontaneous event while making toast one morning – did this mean I was sexually attracted to toasted bread? Or was it the toaster itself? Or the time it happened when I was mowing the lawn – did I now have a thing for lawn mowers?

However, the most embarrassing time occurred when I had a minor role in the usual end-of-term extravaganza. Walking out on stage in front of the whole school with this uncontrollable thing in your pants is not funny. I tried holding my prop – a tennis racket – in order to hide my unwanted activity. However, a tennis racket proved to be an inadequate piece of equipment for the purpose. It became obvious what the cause of my discomfort to the rest of the cast, and the watching audience. Especially when I had to turn side-on to them to deliver my lines. I took a fair amount of ridicule over the next few weeks. Things like, "How did the play go? Hope you didn't find it too hard," or, "Saw you in the play, I thought your acting was a little wooden."

Har de har – oh, how we all laughed.

Something else they decided to miss off our sex education was how dangerous having sex could be. I refer here to the numerous sexually transmitted diseases you could catch if you weren't careful. This activity could be seriously detrimental to one's health and well-being, even fatal if you didn't realise you had caught one of the nastier ones on the list. However, for reasons unknown the powers that be decided to think this information wasn't important enough to be included in the sex education syllabus of nineteen seventy-two.

Nor did they consider it reasonable to include the occurrence of nocturnal emissions – or wet dreams as they are more colloquially known. I had my first incident towards the end of my thirteenth year on Planet Earth. I awoke in the early hours of the morning feeling hot and sweaty only to slowly become aware of this wet feeling. I thought I'd wet myself, until common sense reminded me that wee is not sticky and is considerably wetter. It wasn't funny, I had no idea what had happened, and at age thirteen this was not a subject I wanted to ask my mum about. So, I did nothing, and just worried that something had gone wrong with the machinery. As it did not happen again, I assumed it had all fixed itself and we were good. My mind was finally put to rest when a couple of weeks later Phillip proudly announced he had had a wet dream. After further conversation it all began to make sense.

According to our sex education, there was only one sexuality. Hetero. Sex between males and females was the only type of sex that ever took place. Homosexuality didn't exist according to our education. The first time I read that word was in a book that only gave the explanation as: "A person who prefers the company of their own sex." Nothing about being sexually attracted to the same sex. I was a little over thirteen and reading this I assumed I must be homosexual as I much preferred larking around with my mates than sitting down with a girl to talk about our "feelings". It was only later, when I found out exactly what the term meant that I thought, *Well we've never done that playing football.*

It was a sign of the times. Thankfully things have changed. Everyone should receive a full and comprehensive sex education; everyone should true to themselves and not have to face any prejudice because of the way they live their lives.

Growing up is something you can't escape. It's going to happen regardless of what you may want or do. Part of that process is coping with the changes we all go through. You discover new things, like masturbation. I was fourteen the first time I gave it a go, and it felt great. It was amazing. Afterwards I felt fantastic, I had a warm glow and I was relaxed.

From then on, I would do it at least three times a week, until that fateful day at Scout Camp aged fifteen. After that, I didn't do it as often. I'm pretty sure the others did it as well.

It's all part of growing up, and it's all perfectly normal.

Puberty makes you confused and excited all at once. It brings on changes that can be difficult to deal with; but we all go through it and we all come out the other end as grown adults and usually with our sanity intact.

Ultimately though, puberty sucks. Shaving with a face full of pimples is agony. The mood swings are a pain in the arse, as is the excessive sweating and spontaneous erections. It's all embarrassing and frustrating in equal measure. So, I think the least we lads deserve is an occasional wank to relieve the stress.

9. *What do you mean,*

I've got exams?

Well, here we are. Fifteen and about to enter our final year before joining the sixth form. It seemed that just attending school for the last ten years was not enough proof for prospective employers or universities. Apparently, we also had to prove it by passing some exams.

It was a shocker, I can tell you.

I'm not, I have to confess, the brightest bulb in the fridge. The other three were a lot smarter than me and Mike was smarter than anyone else we had ever met.

I was usually top in History, managed the top five for English, but everything else was a constant struggle to keep up. Maths was better, along with Geography. Both teachers assured me that if I put the work in, I would pass the exam. I didn't have the same level of confidence; parts of Maths were still a foreign language to me.

If we thought we had a lot of homework before, well this was on a different level as the teachers pushed us to achieve all that we could.

Monday morning, we would receive a random event from history; five hundred words for Wednesday, please.

Monday afternoon, provide five hundred words describing the role of Horatio in *Hamlet*.

Tuesday it was five hundred by Thursday for some weird event in Geography, then a further assignment to keep me occupied over the weekend.

Wednesday, we receive a further assignment for History and English, to be handed in on Friday – when we would receive a further request to be completed over the weekend.

Oh, and we also received a sheet of fifty Maths problems to complete over the weekend.

All of this was on top of the homework we needed to complete for Social Studies, Art, Biology, Physics and Chemistry.

That was our lives from the return in September through to April the following year. They did kindly let us have a rest over the Christmas break. My routine consisted of getting up in the mornings at seven, having breakfast while I studied for an hour, shower then school all day, an evening meal then back to the books until about ten that night.

The weekend would be spent completing assignments and reading up on what we needed for Monday's lesson.

Then, suddenly it was January, mock exams time.

We were all informed in explicit terms that these mocks would be carried out in the same manner as if they were the real thing.

You entered the exam in silence, found a seat and waited in silence. The exam paper would be provided face down; any who turned the paper over before instructed would be removed.

Anyone caught talking before, during or after would be removed and their paper destroyed.

Anyone entering the examination after the papers had been turned over would be refused entry.

If you needed the bathroom, you raised your hand and were escorted there and back again.

If you required a question explaining, you raised your hand, and a teacher would get to you as soon as possible.

The English exams were split into three parts; the Literature exam was Monday morning, the Language exam in the afternoon. My oral English would take place on Friday afternoon at one thirty.

All the science exams were split into two parts, theory in the morning and the practical exam in the afternoon.

The rest of the exams consisted of one paper lasting up to three hours.

During the History mock, two people ended up

being ejected for talking, and during the English Literature mock one person received a refusal of entry for turning up after the exam had started.

Two weeks later and they were all over. Then it was a return to the same routine as before. The number of assignments started to reduce as time went on, then in April, we were told that there was no need for us to come to the school until our real exams commenced. If we needed to discuss something regarding the subject, then the teachers would be available. Just call in, they told us. Carry on revising at home.

That's when Mum told me to ease off, keep the weekends free to relax. So, a new routine emerged. Sleep until ten, shower, breakfast, study through the day to six. Evening meal with Mum, an hour in front of the television and study through to ten that night.

Towards the end of April, with about four days left until the first exam one of Mum's oldest friends turned up. He happily informed me that he was under strict instructions from Mum to take me out for the day. He announced that he was taking me for a game of golf.

I may not be the next Jack Nicklas, but for a first attempt, I thought I did alright. I managed to hit the ball in a straight line and over a reasonable distance.

When I got home, Mum had packed all my books away, telling me that if I didn't know it now, I never would. I discovered later that evening that the others had had the same done to them by their mothers. So, we went to the pictures.

There was a film that had been released three years earlier which we all desperately wanted to watch. Mainly due to all the fuss made at the time. It was having a special showing in the city centre, and we managed to get in. Our first X-rated film.

The Exorcist was and still is the most terrifying film I have ever seen. I know by today's standards the film is tame, but for me, it still makes the hairs on the back of my neck stand up. I slept with the light on for the next week.

Monday arrived, bringing with it my Biology exam. Theory in the morning, practical in the afternoon. Tuesday was Physics, Wednesday Chemistry. Theory went well; the Chemistry practical was a complete disaster.

Thursday was Social Studies, Friday brought the Art exam – well, we knew that one wasn't going to be a success.

The weekend was spent revising for History on Monday, then English Language Tuesday morning followed by Geography in the afternoon. Wednesday off, then English Literature Thursday morning followed by the oral in the afternoon.

Then, just as suddenly as it started, it was over. Now I had sixteen weeks until I started in the sixth form, assuming I got the required results.

For the first week, I slept in, met up with the lads. It was weird. I had nothing to do, and the next sixteen weeks stretched in front of me.

By the second week, I thought I would go mad with the boredom.

"You can get a job," Mum suggested. Ha ha ha, very funny.

The following day Mum happily informed me that Carol, her friend who worked for a temping agency, was expecting me for an interview at ten thirty. Naturally, I was overcome with emotion by such an act of kindness and self-sacrifice on Mum's part.

Showered and dressed in a shirt and tie, I turned up for the interview. I was in their offices for the next four hours.

First, as I hadn't got my results, I was given an English and Maths test.

Then I filled in lots of bits of paper.

Then I had the actual interview.

They told me they had nothing suitable. They would be in touch if anything turned up.

I went home thinking that was an immense waste of time.

The temping agency called the following Friday. I was told I could start with a small financial services office in the city centre as they needed an office junior – and they wanted to pay me the princely sum of two pounds and ten pence per hour.

I told Mum when she came home; she promptly burst into tears and complained that I was growing up too fast. Honestly, this was all her idea, and now she was moaning about it. I offered to turn it down, at which point Mum asked me politely where I was going live.

I took the hint and dutifully reported to the office the following Monday.

It turns out the title of office junior is another term for general dogsbody. Someone to make the tea and fetch and carry. Still, I worked out I would be earning the life-changing amount of three hundred and thirty-six pounds a month. Mum told me she would have seventy-five of it for my keep. I now suspected that her actions might not have been as altruistic as I first thought.

My friends thought it was hilarious that I had a job until they realised how much money I was getting. They made appointments the next day. Two weeks later we all had jobs.

It didn't take long to get into the routine of a working life. I would arrive at the office at eight-thirty in the morning, sign in, collect everyone's cups from around the office, fill the kettle and make the morning tea or coffee.

Then I would wander over to my desk, pick up whatever filing had been left from the previous day and put it where it needed to go. I would spend most of the rest of the day working through file requests as they arrived, delivering them to whoever ordered them and ensuring there was a constant flow of drinks.

It was, as you can see, a very important job that carried a huge amount of responsibility.

I bought my first clothes, including a new suit, out of my first month's wages. This action produced another flood of tears from Mother, although not as much as the following month when I arrived home with a bunch of flowers, a box of chocolates and the announcement that I was taking her out for dinner.

Although, to be perfectly honest that wasn't of my own doing. Aunty Pam had been dropping not so subtle hints ever since she found out I had a job.

Then, just a suddenly it was July, our exam results were ready to be picked up. We all went in together, joined the queue and picked up our little white envelopes containing our future. Other students stood around reading their results. There were tears and smiles in equal measure.

The four of us found a quiet corner, looked nervously at each other, counted to three and ripped open the envelope. I had to read the information twice to make sure:

English	B+
History	A+
Maths	B-
Social Studies	A
Physics	C
Chemistry	D
Biology	B-
Technical Drawing	C
Art	C

WOW – I had done a lot better in a couple of subjects than I had expected. More importantly, I had the grades to do A-Levels in History, English and Social Studies.

Isaac's grades were slightly better, Phillip's around the same and, as expected Mike got straight As in everything.

Phillip mentioned he had a couple of bottles of wine in his bag to help us celebrate. The idea was met with varying degrees of enthusiasm. Congregating at the park, we proceeded to pass the bottles around, enjoying our success. At some point I needed to pee. I stood up, the world started spinning, and I dashed into the bushes to throw up.

The others were not far behind me.

It was horrible. Lying down and feeling like I needed to hold on to something. We couldn't go home like this; Mike said we could all go to his as the house was empty. So, we all crashed out in his lounge.

Mum called Mike's house a couple of hours later, so I went home. I passed her the results, and I assumed she was pleased from the scream of delight she let out. Which was unfortunate as the Grand National Horse Race was currently taking place in my head.

Mum told me to go to bed, adding that she hoped this would put me off drinking forever. It didn't.

10. (No) Sex, (No) Drugs,

Just Rock and Roll.

Being born in Liverpool it is generally assumed that you are going to be a Beatles fan. It is written into the constitution of the city. It was just expected, and since their break-up the city has been on the lookout for the next Beatles.

Then, in nineteen seventy-six, four twelve-year-old lads came along. They won ITV's talent show New Faces. Calling themselves 'Our Kid' they had a hit record, 'You Just Might See Me Cry'. The fuss made around them was extraordinary; they were interviewed on the local North West news programme, the city's media did indeed hail them as the next Beatles. Twelve months later they had vanished, just a flash in the pan, and are now largely forgotten. Sorry lads, but there is never going to be another Beatles. They were and remain quite simply unique.

Music in the mid to late seventies seemed to have lost its way a little. For example:

Brotherhood of Man had just won the Eurovision Song Contest with their sentimental number 'Save Your Kisses For Me'.

Dolly Parton had had a hit with her song 'Jolene'.

The Bay City Rollers were at the height of their popularity, which would begin to recede over the next year.

We still had The Who, The Rolling Stones and Queen.

The Beatles were no more, and the Liverpool music scene – which has always been ahead of the rest of the country – was determined to move away from the Merseybeat label.

It was time for a revolution in the music industry, which had grown stagnant, churning out the same old material over and over – or at least that was the feeling of most young people.

A new sound was emerging, a brand of music that would grab sensationalist headlines and upset the establishment. It would cause shock and disgust, and the condemnation of our parents and the country's press.

Punk Rock was coming.

The seventies were subject to a period of huge political unrest. Edward Heath had lost the nineteen seventy-four election following the miners' strike. From January through to the election in March that year, commercial businesses had been limited to the use of electricity to three consecutive days a week only – the infamous three-day week as it soon became known.

Labour won the election, James Callaghan was the new Prime Minister. By nineteen seventy-six the country was heading into what the press called 'The Winter of Discontent'. During this period there was widespread strike action in both the private and public sectors. Trade unions were demanding higher and higher pay rises while the government was desperately trying to control inflation that would rise to an unprecedented thirty per cent.

The country was suffering from a combination of two miners' strikes in as many years, an energy crisis, a financial crash and an embarrassing warranty from the International Monetary Fund. There were over one million people unemployed, the highest since the depression of the nineteen twenties. The United Kingdom of Great Britain was broke, the youth of the country felt betrayed. They expressed the sense of disloyalty through their music.

Punk Rock was coming.

The only place in Liverpool to see these new bands was at Eric's Club situated in the world-famous Matthew Street.

However, we were only sixteen. We weren't allowed into clubs.

Then Eric's did something no other club had ever done. They introduced a junior membership for sixteen- to eighteen-year-olds. It was an incredible break from the norm. For an annual membership of fifty pence, you could pay your entrance fee of a pound and attend the Saturday matinee.

Any band booked to play a Saturday night were expected to play the Saturday Matinee as well.

The first ever band to play were The Stranglers.

The second week it was The Runaways.

In the third week, Eric's played host to the now iconic Sex Pistols.

We missed them all. It wasn't until week four that we became members. Glenn Matlock, formerly of the Sex Pistols, was headlining with his new band Rich Kids. We wanted to see a real live Sex Pistol.

For the first time of what would become a regular Saturday afternoon event, the four of us entered the hallowed rooms of Eric's. Walking down the stairs you entered the bar area (as this was for the youth membership, they only served soft drinks). Holding tightly on to our bottles of Coke, we passed through the doors at the end of the bar into another world.

The world of anarchy, protest and revolution.

It was here that the real Punk Rockers hung out. We looked around; it soon became evident that we were overdressed for the event. Lads and girls wore torn jeans, t-shirts with swear words on, safety pins through earlobes, noses, cheeks, and lips. Their hair was dyed with bright, sometimes fluorescent colours. No more long hair, you either carried a Mohican, or it was cropped.

Filled with excitement and anticipation, we looked around and took all of it in. It had taken us a while to convince our parents. However, there had been no trouble reported in the local press since the club opened, which we think was the final convincer and made our parents feel more comfortable with the idea. Once one parent agreed, the others soon followed.

We were sixteen, and Eric's was providing us with a place to be part of something. To belong in a society that had managed to destroy any future for its youth, had largely written them off.

Eventually the support band came onto the stage. The lead singer walked up to the mic stand and said the immortal words, "Hello, we're Joy Division."

Don't ask me what they played, it's too long ago now. We have all been fans since that day in late nineteen seventy-six.

Then we watched Rich Kid perform.

It was unbelievably loud. The only time we had experienced loud music was at the school end-of-term disco. These noise levels were on another level; when they finished my ears still buzzed for a good ten minutes after.

What's more, they all came out into the bar to chat and sign autographs.

It was, we all agreed, the best time ever. Until the next week when we saw The Clash, supported by an unknown band called The Specials.

Over the next two years, we saw The Jam, Souxie and the Banshees, The Boomtown Rats, Tom Robinson and his Band, The Stranglers, Blondie, Stiff Little Fingers, Buzzcocks, and Ian Drury to name a few.

We eventually got to see the Sex Pistols, and they performed the record that gained them their notoriety

– God Save the Queen.

I have been to a number of concerts since those days, but Eric's holds a very special place.

11. A Secret Revealed

The four of us had been friends for years, we had virtually lived in each other's pockets all our lives. There wasn't anything we didn't know about each other – or so we all thought.

It was a Saturday afternoon in the summer. No different to any other. A trip to the cinema to see some new film called Star Wars was planned, followed by a bite to eat.

We watched this genre-changing movie in the Woolton Picture House. It was a very enjoyable romp of a film, we all thoroughly enjoyed it. However, it was just another science-fiction film; none of us thought it was going to have the impact on the consciousness of youth that it went on to have. We just thought it was a fun film to watch.

After the film, we all walked over to the Ying Wah Chinese restaurant to eat. We liked this establishment, mainly because we were only seventeen and they didn't ask awkward questions when we ordered a beer. Plus, the food was nice. As usual, we ordered the banquet.

At first the conversation centred around our thoughts on the film we had just watched. No-one else really knew who Alec Guinness was – I confess I only knew because Mum was a fan; as a result I had seen him in The Lavender Hill Mob, The Man in the White Suit and various other Ealing comedies. Years later he would be the epitome of a Cold War warrior in the BBC adaption of John le Carré's *Tinker, Tailor, Soldier, Spy*. Then it was the usual talk around football, school work and which girls we fancied in the sixth form.

I mentioned I was considering asking Julie Shields out, which received the usual suggestive seventeen-year-old comments. Phillip then said, "Maybe you will finally lose your virginity."

Which is when I made the confession about Anya and the Scout camp two years previously. All three of them stared at me in astonishment, I suspect because this was the first time I had mentioned it. That was when Phillip admitted he had done the same with Bridget.

Isaac, somewhat red-faced confessed that he had done it in the February half term on holiday with his family.

Mike was quiet.

We all looked at him; he just looked back uncomfortably.

Phillip asked him the question. Mike chewed his bottom lip and looked even more uncomfortable.

Phillip offered to fix him up, naming a couple of girls he knew fancied him. He was really making a big thing about it, which I think is why Mike lost patience and told him that he did not need 'fixing up' as he had lost his virginity the previous month.

We all pressed him for details, after all we had given names, times and places and a detailed description of how it had happened. Mike became agitated; it was obvious he did not want to give any details. However, Phillip was his usual persistent self. "Just a name," he asked.

Which is when we heard five simple words, five words that sent our world spiralling into unknown territory.

"Peter, his name is Peter."

Well, whatever we had been expecting, it wasn't that. It certainly brought the conversation to a standstill.

Then we all tried to talk at once.

Isaac pleaded for silence, then asked Mike if he was telling us what we thought he was telling us. Mike just nodded, staring at the table cloth. I asked if he was sure. Mike said he had been sure since he was fourteen.

It is fair to say that we were all stunned by what Mike had just told us.

Phillip was positively shocked; his reaction on that day is not something he has ever been proud of. Unfortunately, the macho sportsman in him took over control of both his brain and his mouth. I know he regretted how he reacted as soon as it was done, and for the rest of his life he was always ashamed of his behaviour that day.

As for Isaac and me? Well... I think we looked at Mike as though he had just arrived from another planet.

Mike looked at the three of us; you could see the tears in his eyes at our reactions. He stood up and left. For me, and all of us, our eternal regret on that day is that we did not get up and follow him and bring him back. He needed us to support him as friends should, and we let him down badly.

The three of us dealt with this revelation in our own way over the next couple of days. In the end only one thing mattered.

Michael was our friend, nothing else mattered, and I for one did not want to lose that friendship. Isaac and Phillip felt the same way, so we all went around to Mike's house to see if he fancied a kick around in the park.

The look of relief on his face when he saw all three of us standing there told us everything. He had been worrying about losing his closest, and essentially his only, friends. By calling round, we were letting him know we didn't care about his sexual preferences, that all that mattered was a friendship that went back over our whole lives.

As we walked over to the park, Phillip pulled Mike to one side and was extremely contrite in his apology. He was visibly upset and ashamed at what he had said. Mike did what he always did after any disagreement between us, told him to forget it. It was in the past, today was a new day with new beginnings.

As they re-joined us, Isaac asked, "Peter who?" After extracting promises of confidentiality on pain of death, Mike told us. No wonder he wanted it kept quiet. None of us thought the headmaster would react well to that piece of information regarding his eldest son.

After that, the subject never came up, and although things would never be exactly as they had been, a sense of normality returned to the group dynamics.

Until a year later. We had just finished our A-Levels, waiting for our results in anticipation of going off to university a couple of months later. It was because of this that Mike decided to tell his parents, which just confirmed to me that Mike was the bravest person I knew.

It did not go well.

His mum was upset, naturally.

His dad, however, went ballistic. I mean on a nuclear scale. At first his dad treated it as a joke, just not a very funny one. Then as he came to a realisation that his son was not joking, he threw him out. Just like that. Telling him that, "There is no place in his house for a shirt-lifting, queer little arse bandit."

Which is when I gained a roommate. University was about ten weeks away, it just made sense. Where else was he going to go? Isaac and Phillip's houses had no room. For us, it was just Mum and me.

I admit, I didn't know what I was going to tell

Mum, other than Mike had been kicked out. When we both went down to talk to her, she looked at Mike and just said, "You've come out to your dad, haven't you?"

She said she had suspected for the last year. Then she told Mike he would always be welcome in her house, and of course he could stay. She also told Mike that, "Sorry, but your dad has always been a prick." It was first and only time I heard Mum use bad language.

We went around and picked up his stuff the next day after his dad had left for work; all of us helped him move. Phillip had borrowed his mum's car, having passed his test a couple of weeks earlier.

The news that Mike was now living at mine soon spread. When we met other members of the upper sixth, they would ask questions. Our stance was always the same, it's none of your business – it's a private matter between Mike and his parents.

It seemed to work, but rumours started to circulate about Mike's sexuality. We all defended him, denying any such thing.

I appreciate that this may seem wrong, but this was

nineteen seventy-eight. Homophobia was a real, tangible thing. Men got beaten up and worse for being gay. There's no point in denying it, it was a different time – that doesn't make it right or make such behaviour acceptable. However, Mike had only just turned eighteen. Sex between gay men wasn't permitted if you were under twenty-one. So, it was also about keeping Mike safe.

Two years later there would be a bigger debate about homosexuality – and it would take part on national television. Because, in two years the AIDS epidemic would hit the headlines, which at first just fed the homophobia and just proved to the lunatic Christian right wing what they had always said. That was until the first case involving a heterosexual couple, then the whole thing took on a new dynamic.

Mike's mum would sneak round for coffee and cake and to talk to her son. She reconciled herself to the fact that her son was gay. Over the years their relationship became stronger. His mum would often visit him at university.

His parents split within the year. His dad always

blamed Mike for the split, refusing to meet or speak to him. Mike tried, he offered several olive branches, he always sent birthday and Christmas cards – receiving none in return. At least his dad didn't mark the cards 'return to sender', Mike used to say; which always gave him hope of a final reconciliation.

12. Sixth Form and Beyond

Life as a sixth former was completely different.

We stuck out like a sore thumb dressed in the blue blazers of the sixth form. We are now considered to be elder statesmen of the school. Expected to carry ourselves with some decorum. "Remember, the younger student looks to you as an example." Well, the younger students were in trouble then. Especially after the head of the sixth form was caught shagging a third-year girl in the toilets after the third-year summer disco, which he was attending as a chaperone!

We only had to attend registration on a Monday

and a Friday morning. Other than that, we were left to our own devices. Provided we turned up to classes, got our assignments in on time, we were left alone. We were even allowed to smoke within the confines of the sixth form common room.

This common room came equipped with a hot and cold drinks machine, a snack machine, darts board, and pool table. It was more like a youth club than a school common room.

It was a very different world, and the teachers treated us like adults.

It was good we had somewhere to relax because the workload was even heavier than before. Out of the three, O-Levels, A-Levels and a degree, A-Levels are the absolute worse.

I was studying four subjects – English, History, Social Studies, and the obligatory General Studies, and the workload was off the scales. How Mike was coping with the same subjects, plus Maths and Law, was a mystery.

I had an hour of English every Monday and Wednesday morning and a two-hour slot last thing on

Friday. After each lesson I would be required to produce an essay critiquing the passage we had just read, using quotes from the text to support my argument. It was the same for History.

However, Social Studies was lighter, and for General Studies we were required to read the papers at the weekend to prepare for the discussion on Monday afternoon.

I managed most of it, but to be honest I didn't then and still don't know why T S Eliot considered April to be the cruellest month. Or why Steinbeck's *East of Eden* is supposed to be a commentary on the fall of man.

So yet again all our time was taken up with study. Except for Saturday afternoons in Eric's. Those times were considered sacrosanct and were probably the main reason none of us went mad.

Teachers no longer reminded us when assignments were due; if you needed more time it was your responsibility to negotiate the new deadline with the teacher – which was always an interesting proceeding.

There was one lesson that we all came to detest.

Friday mornings, straight after registration we had a lesson with the headmaster. During the first of these sessions, he informed us that this was a time for us to discuss life, world problems, and politics – or any topic we wanted to discuss.

At first, it all seemed to be going well. Everyone took him at his word and joined in enthusiastically. In the beginning, these conversations on our part would be simplistic. However, as time passed, we all became better at getting a point across, which now I look back might have been the whole point of the exercise.

Mike, however, was beginning to show the early signs as to why he would become a defence barrister nobody would relish opposing. Within weeks he could hold his own with the headmaster, take any point he made, turn it on its head and throw it back at him. I am slightly ashamed to say that when Mike started to speak most of us kept quiet, we hunted as a pack – with Mike as our alpha wolf.

Everyone knew when Mike had won the day. The headmaster would dismiss Mike's argument with a wave of his hand and then give us a speech about listening to the radicals in society. Mike wasn't the only one he did this with, the problem was, sadly, that a significant number of the upper sixth form where just cleverer.

As the years in the sixth form progressed these sessions became a glorious waste of time as they descended into us all sitting in silence while the headmaster lectured us on whatever had annoyed him that week.

However, life in the sixth form wasn't just hard work. I mean, we had extra responsibilities as ambassadors of the school, we were always on duty for parents' evenings to act as guides. We did the same each year for the visiting prospective new pupils. We would also be drafted in to chaperone each of the annual end-of-year summer discos for each year.

Life was hectic, but we had fun as well. The whole sixth form took over a local bowling alley one night; we had a trip to Blackpool Pleasure Beach, or a night out to see a new release at the cinema.

Occasionally we would gather at someone's house for a couple of illicit drinks and, very rarely, a bit of sex. I had three on-off relationships during my time in the sixth form – all of which ended amicably and none of which I regretted. Sex was just something we did, no-one wanted a serious relationship – no-one had the time, to be fair. Most of the boys in the sixth form carried a condom in their wallet.

I also tried smoking again, still didn't like it. I tried pot, which just made me dizzy and throw up, so I didn't see the point. That was the end of my drug experimentation, even during my years at university.

The best thing we all did though was when I finally got to have a go at paintballing!

Paintballing had suddenly become the thing to do as young adults. From nothing, this pastime had exploded onto the scene from nowhere. As a result, a paintballing day for the winner and twenty friends was offered as a prize on a local radio station's competition. I have no recollection what you had to do to win, but Richard Osbourne, a fellow sixth former, won it. He promptly invited the whole of the lower sixth.

The facility we used was on the outskirts of Huyton. Isaac's mum kindly dropped us all off. The first hour was spent going through the required health and safety and rules bit; masks must be worn at all times when in the war zone; minimum distance you are allowed to shoot from is fifteen feet – any closer could cause serious injury; a hit is only counted if the paintball bursts and leaves a mark on the other player's body; once a player has been hit, you cannot continue to shoot him.

We obeyed the bit about keeping the masks on and the minimum distance; after that, anyone was fair game.

Once we were introduced to the equipment, that was it. We all changed into the boiler suits provided, but on our masks and off we went.

A siren sounded to signify the start of the game. I ran for my life and dived behind the nearest bunker. I managed to reach it without being shot; ten seconds later Isaac landed beside me.

The idea of the game was simple, survive. Isaac and I teamed up to take out as many of the others as possible. Isaac got the first kill when someone thought they could sneak past and come up behind us. Isaac took him out with enthusiasm.

My first kill came about five minutes later. I saw some movement out the corner of my eye, turned around and just fired and killed one of my best friends. I don't think Phillip has ever forgiven me.

The game progressed along similar lines. Eventually both of us were caught in an ambush and were shot a dozen times between us. We retired to the cabins and enjoyed a mug of hot chocolate and a bacon sandwich.

It was great fun; all of us were hyped up from the experience as well as tired and filthy. My body stung from the number of hits I had received, and all my muscles ached from the efforts. I was astonished when I returned home and stripped off to shower at the number of bruises that were beginning to appear all over.

A part of our lives was ending, the end of an era.

Universities were inviting us to visit, our futures were taking shape, at least for the next three to four years. Things were changing, and it would not be long before the four of us went off in different directions.

Mike had already received an unconditional offer from Oxford to study law.

Isaac had been offered a place in Leeds to study English provided he got the required grades.

Phillip had decided not to go to university, saying that he'd had enough of education. He had received an offer of a junior position working for the media department of Liverpool Football Club, which was a dream come true. The references he got from his teachers helped. When he showed them to me, I didn't recognise the person they were writing about.

And me? I'd taken up an offer from Nottingham university to study History.

The whole of the upper sixth had a celebration at the end of term and met up again in the local pub after collecting our results in August nineteen seventy-eight.

The four of us had one last hurrah in the last week of September. We laughed a lot, drank too much and swore we would always be friends. The next day, Mike left for Oxford.

Four became three, then two as Isaac set off.

Then, the following week I left for Nottingham. I can't begin to imagine how difficult this must have been for Phillip, as the one left behind. We had all been friends for the best part of fifteen years. I know I would miss them all, it was a painful change at first. It took time, but I soon made new friends in university, but none of them were like those three guys. They were my best friends in the world and would remain so.

The relationship between us would change over the years as we started work, fell in and out of love, got married, had kids, got divorced.

That was just life stuff, but the essential friendship built on over years of misadventures was the best.

During the next thirty years we remained friends. I was Phillip's best man at his wedding, and a shoulder to lean on when he divorced. He is now the Head of Media for LFC.

Isaac abandoned his degree in English. Instead, he went on to study as a Rabbi. None of us had seen that one coming. He is happily married to Sarah and has three boys. He lives in Milton Keynes.

I became a History Teacher; back where it all started in Halewood. I run the History department for the same secondary school we all attended. Like Phillip I'm divorced. I wanted children, she didn't. I was happy being a teacher; she was, it turned out, not happy about my being happy to be a teacher.

Mike gained a first in law from Oxford and was offered a place at a very prestigious law chamber in London. He was never reconciled with his dad. He may have been in future years, however, that chance was taken from him when, ten years later at age forty-one, Mike was killed by a hit-and-run driver.

I still look back on those formative years with great fondness.

Last month the three of us were back together for the wedding of Isaac's eldest son.

Whenever we get together, since we lost him, we raise a glass of single malt whiskey to Mike's memory. Always a sixteen-year-old Laphroig.

It was his favourite.

ABOUT THE AUTHOR

John Hawksworth is fourteen (actually he is middle aged – he just refuses to grow up).

After finishing school (not literally a 'finishing school') he decided to qualify as the worst salesman in Great Britain. He was truly terrible. So, he decided to become the head barman in the Eagle and Child pub (which he says is a whole other book on its own).

Eventually he was offered a chance to work in the pensions and life insurance business. It having been his lifelong ambition to work in the finance industry, he accepted their offer and spent the next twenty years working as a compliance officer.

He lives in Liverpool with his wife and son.

He has climbed the three peaks, canoed down Ben Nevis and jumped out of three perfectly serviceable airplanes for reasons best known to himself. He is considering a new fitness regime, to which he has downloaded the 'Couch to 5K' app. Whether he will do anything further remains to be seen.

He is a committed Christian and attends his local church as often as work and life allows.

Printed in Great Britain
by Amazon

38063780R00090